# HENRIE'S HERO HUNT

HOUSE OF HEROES

# HENRIE'S HERO HUNT

**Petra James**

**Illustrations by A. Yi**

**Kane Miller**
A DIVISION OF EDC PUBLISHING

First American Edition 2021
Kane Miller, A Division of EDC Publishing

Text © 2020 Petra James
Illustrations © 2020 A. Yi
Published by arrangement with Walker Books Limited, London.
First published in 2020 by Walker Books Australia Pty Ltd.

For information contact:
Kane Miller, A Division of EDC Publishing
5402 S. 122nd E. Ave, Tulsa, OK 74146
**www.kanemiller.com**
**www.myubam.com**

Library of Congress Control Number: 2021930341

Printed and bound in the United States of America
1 2 3 4 5 6 7 8 9 10

ISBN: 978-1-68464-355-4

*To Steph, Julie & Kath.*

*Best sisters.*

# What's happened so far?

**HELLO, I'M HENRIE.** You might know me from *Hapless Hero Henrie* but don't worry if you don't. Here are the important bits:

**Me, Henrie Melchior:** dramatic birth, missing parents, mysterious note.

**Ellie:** ingenious aunt with the eyes of an eagle, the teeth of a beaver and the heart of a lion.

Ellie told me to write that. I thought the beaver bit was over the top, but she said small rodents with iron teeth pack a punch.

**Alex Fischer:**
tall boy, available on the spot for an adventure.

**Albert Abernathy:**
Grandfather's private secretary. Kidnapper.

Alex and I followed some splots and stowed away on the Melchior jet. He disappeared and I had a bumpy meeting with my uncle and cousins. Girls aren't welcome in the House of Melchior (long story). My grandfather Octavia Melchior was happy to see me but I can't talk about him at the moment. (Later, maybe.) The Melchiors locked me in a room but Ellie found me. We were trapped in a fire with Alex and his Super Sleuth dad but we found a secret doorway and Octavia's will, and sent the measly Melchiors packing. Ellie and I were packing too when a note within a note led us to the Control Center, the heart of HoMe, and the Hero Hotline. We were walking out the door when the Hero Hotline started ringing, shrill in the quiet around us. Brave thoughts rushed toward me faster than a bullet train and I picked up the Hero Hotline.

I'm holding it right now.

## Chapter One

# Is There a Hero at HoMe?

**MY BRAIN WAS** screaming at me:

**WHY DID YOU PICK UP THE HERO HOTLINE?**

Brains can be really loud but, I had to admit, it had a point. I was asking myself the same thing: Why did I pick up the Hero Hotline? Me. Hapless Hero Henrie. The first girl born into the House of Heroes in 200 years. Only *heroes* were allowed to answer the Hero Hotline.

What was I thinking?

### Note to you

Sometimes it's better not to think. Thoughts can burrow deep into the dark of you and refuse to come out for days, weeks, months, years ... EVER.
**PS** They can start to stink.

I had come to the House of Melchior to find my mum and dad but found instead that Octavia Melchior had told them I was ... **dead.**

### Note to you

I'm the very definition of alive. Put your hand on your heart. Can you feel it beat, beat, beating? Mine feels like that too.

Ellie and I were going to turn the world inside out to find my mum and dad.

Not tomorrow. Not the day after. Not the day after the day after the day after. But right **now.**

We were about to catch a plane home.

We didn't have time to answer a call for help.

But even as that thought slammed through me, it whipped around and a bubble of doubt fizzed up.

*Oh, no.* My head was a tumble jumble.

I looked at Ellie. Ellie looked at me.

I knew what she was thinking.

I knew she knew what I was thinking.

What Ellie was thinking:

We haven't got time to answer a call for help.

What I was thinking:

Have we got time to answer a call for help?

## Note to you

Okay, so maybe this "I know what you're thinking" thing is not 100 percent reliable but don't lose hope. Test it out with a friend. Think of something and ask him or her to think of something. Are you thinking the same thing?

13

◯ Yes

WOW! That's amazing. You've got potential. I'll tell
Claire Voyant* about you.

◯ No

Don't despair. Make it the best of three.


It was like a slo-mo moment in the movies when
everything unsaid floats up to the top of your head –
looking for a way out.

Who is it?

**No**.

What do they want?

**Yes.**

We have to go.

Why?

**Help.**

What?

The *ring, ring, ring* of the Hero Hotline had pulled
me toward it like a sleepwalker. But I had woken
with a start. All those brave thoughts that had sent

---

* Claire Voyant could do with some help. She'd told my
mum I was going to be a boy.


14

*pick-it-up pick-it-up pick-it-up* signals to my hand were long gone. And I knew why. They'd found themselves all alone in a place they didn't belong.

**Inside non-hero me.**

### Note to you

Don't make Courage too comfy when it arrives. It never stays for long — even if you bolt the front door, shut all the windows and feed it french fries with homemade ketchup.

Ellie pointed to the phone in my hand. "Well, are you going to answer it?"

I looked at the phone in confusion. "Me?" I said.

My palms were sweaty. I wiped them on my T-shirt.

"Yes, you," said Ellie. "You picked it up."

"I know," I said, "but it's the Hero Hotline. I'm not a hero."

"Are you sure?" said Ellie, looking at me with her "I'm-thinking-deep-thoughts-here" face. Her eyebrows joined forces at times like this and looked like a seagull about to swoop.

"Finn and Carter said I wasn't," I said. "They told me I didn't belong here."

My cousins had disliked me as soon as I'd arrived at the House of Melchior.

But that was okay because I'd disliked *them* as soon as *I'd* arrived at the House of Melchior. And nothing they did after this made me like them any more. Although Finn and I maybe could have become friends if we'd had longer to get to know each other. *And* if Carter hadn't been around. But my uncle Caspian said loyalty to the family was everything. Finn would always be thick with Carter. It was in his DNA.

Caspian and the boys had disappeared pretty quickly after the fire and the discovery of Octavia's will. But Ellie *had* threatened to call the police so I guess that would make even me move faster than usual.

"Those two," said Ellie, snorting. "Are you really going to let their words stick to you?"

I knew Ellie wasn't going to wait for me to answer that question.

### Note to you

Some questions aren't really questions. They look like questions and sound like questions but they're just pretending to be questions.

When Ellie was hot under the collar, she was a steamroller of words. I knew she'd be steaming in less than five seconds.

**5**
**4**
**3**
**2 ...**

"Being born into a house of heroes doesn't make you a hero," said Ellie. She was red in the face now, a volcano of emotion. "Did Finn and Carter ever do anything heroic?"

I thought.

I didn't have to think for long.

short thought

I shook my head.

*Nope.*

"Don't let other people tell you who you are or who you can be, Henrie," said Ellie. "That's for you to work out."

Ellie's words buzzed through me. *A hero? Me? Could I be?* I had to admit "Hero Henrie" sounded heaps better than "Hapless Hero Henrie." And you know how much I like alliteration (and raspberry-jam sandwiches and salted caramels).

"You're smart and fearless, Henrie," said Ellie. "And don't you forget it." She nodded at the phone in my hand again. "Well?"

I looked at it in surprise. I'd almost forgotten I was holding it so I bet you had too.

If *I* was on the other end of this phone, I'd never wait eight pages for someone to answer. I'd be dunking a pink marshmallow in hot chocolate and reading Harry Potter by now.

## Question to you

Have you waited eight pages?

◯ Yes          ◯ No

The person on the other end must really need a hero.

I gulped. And they were about to get … **me.**

I opened my mouth and **la la la**-ed like we did in drama class to make our vocal cords braver, and put the phone up to my ear.

In my best hero voice, I uttered that famous hero word:

"Hello?"

# Chapter Two

# The Sound of Silence

**THERE WAS SILENCE** on the other end of the phone. Not even a **HELLO** back.

I frowned. That was unusual.

**Note to you**
HELLO is like a yawn, bow or sneeze. It makes you hello, yawn, bow or sneeze back.

It's funny how noisy silence can be. I could hear the *swooshing* of free-flowing air, hurtling through satellites in space and telecommunication cables, waiting to breathe into spoken words. I couldn't even hear the other person breathing. But that was okay. I was breathing loud enough for both of us.

*Note to you*
*I'd never realized how hard it is to think and breathe*
*and speak at the same time. You should try it.*

"Say something else," said Ellie.

"HoMe's Hero Hotline. Can I help you?"

**Whoa!** Listen to me. I sounded super official. I was impressing me so I bet the person on the other end was really impressed too.

**The Hero's Handbook**
**Top Tip 11:** Try to sound official even when you don't feel official.

Maybe the person was too impressed to speak?

That happened to me on speech day when Jack Margate gave a talk on electrical engineering. It was full of long words, like "Peripheral Component Interconnect" and "Tachometer" and even Mr. Tribble had to look up some of the words in the dictionary.

"Congratulations, Jack," Mr. Tribble had said. "That was fabulously incomprehensible. I'll be sure to congratulate your father at the next parent–teacher night."

When I got home, I'd told Ellie I had to change my surname immediately.

Speaking after Jack Margate for the rest of my school life was going to be bad for my health.

"Nothing," I whispered to Ellie who was now pressed close, listening in.

"They might be shy," she whispered back. "Or scared."

"I'm not scared," said a voice on the other end of the phone.

Ellie and I jumped. A speaker had spoken.

## Note to you

Whispers can be louder than you think.

It was a girl's voice.

"You took so long to answer I thought you'd fallen asleep," she said.

I nodded. She had a point. I know I kept you all waiting too but I had a lot to think about.

The girl *said* she wasn't scared but sometimes what you say and how you say it don't quite match. She sounded scared to me. Her words were wobbly. And kind of high. Not quite a squeak but they definitely had squeaky potential.

"Can I help you?" I said.

"Yes," she said.

I waited but she didn't say anything else.

"Well, you've rung the right place," I said. "HELP

22

is our middle name." I paused. That sounded good but what should I say next? Then I spied the Hero Hotline Help Ledger.

I should get a few details.

I opened it to a new page and grabbed a pen. "What kind of help do you need?" I said.

"I don't know," she said.

"Oh," I said.

"What did she say?" whispered Ellie.

"She said she doesn't know what kind of help she needs," I whispered back.

"Who are you talking to?" said the squeaky girl.

"Ellie," I said.

"Who's Ellie?" said the girl.

"My aunt," I said. "She's listening in."

"Oh," said the girl. "Do you trust her?"

"Yes," I said. "With my life."

As I said those three words, I suddenly felt how truly enormous they were. An avalanche of emotions hit me in the heart.

When Ellie had read the note pinned to the pomegranate after Alex and I'd gone to meet Albert Abernathy at Poole Street Station, she'd dropped everything and raced around the world to find me. Even though she'd disappeared down the chute in the wardrobe pretty soon after, she'd turned up in the old factory quarters again when I needed her most. Ellie **chomped** on danger. She *was* like a beaver.

Ellie had said she'd turn the world upside down to find me.

I knew I'd do the same for her.

I smiled at Ellie and she smiled back.

This time I *knew* we were thinking the same thing.

"You might trust her," said the girl, "but how do I know I can trust *you*?"

"You don't," I said. "That's the thing about trust. It's like hope. You have to close your eyes and leap toward it."

"Easy for you to say," she said.

"I'm not just saying it," I said. "I know it."

24

"How do you know it?" she said.

"I met a stranger a few days ago," I said. "A boy called Alex Fischer. And I didn't know I could trust him. Until I did."

Alex Fischer had turned out to be pretty okay for a tall boy.

Okay, I know what you're thinking.

You're thinking: *but he didn't tell you his Super Sleuth dad had been hired by your grandfather to find your mum and dad.*

And you're right. He didn't. And that was a Big Thing not to tell me.

But everything was happening so fast in the present we didn't have time to piece together the past of us. That came later. When we found Octavia's will and discovered he'd left everything to me and Alex and his dad.

"Is this Alex there too?" she said.

"No, he's with his dad," I said. "Ellie and I are meeting up with them tomorrow."

"I wish I was with my dad," said the girl. "He's at a paleontology conference in Bolivia. They've just discovered the bones of a baby T. rex from the late Cretaceous period."

Lucky I was working my way through the *ologies* in the dictionary and knew how to spell *paleontology*.

Big words can slow you down when you're taking fast notes.

## A few of my favorite ologies

**brontology:** the study of thunder

**garbology:** the study of garbage (best on trash day when streets stew with smell)

**limacology:** the study of slugs.

I ♡ SLUGS

Brought to you by the
Slug Appreciation Society

**nephology:** the study of clouds

"Is that why you need help?" I said. "It's something to do with your dad?"

"No," she said. "It's something else."

That was one of the longest sentences she'd said so I figured she was on a word roll. But silence and breathing filled the phone again.

I knew some people had trouble finding their words but not me. Ellie said I even talk in my sleep. I laugh sometimes too. There's always interesting stuff going on in my head. With or without me.

"Try beginning in the middle," I said. Mr. Tribble said if you couldn't start at the very beginning, the middle was the next best spot.

"I didn't even know what it was," she said.

"You didn't even know what *what* was?" I said, frowning. There were middles and middles. This was the middle of the middle.

"*Psst*, Henrie," whispered Ellie.

I looked up.

Ellie had found a Hero Mobile Phone on top of the cabinet, next to the Hero Hotline. She held it up to show me the screen. It had a landline tracker on it. Brilliant. I knew the drill. We had to keep the girl talking long enough for us to get a fix on her location.

"You didn't even know what *what* was?" I repeated.

27

"What I saw," she said.

"Okay, good, you saw something," I said. "What did you see?"

"Someone following me," she said. "A girl, I think."

"How did you know a girl – you think – was following you?" I said.

"I'm stuck inside a lot these days," she said, "and I'd been looking out the window. I'm on the third floor so there's a good view of the street. I'd seen this girl outside, leaning against the lamppost and then I saw her walking behind us when I went to my Spanish class at the Language Center."

"Are you sure she was following you?" I said. "It could have been a coincidence."

"There are no such things as coincidences," she said. "Penelope Fuggleton says so."

"Who's Penelope Fuggleton?" I said.

"Only the author of the best kid detective stories in the world," she said. "I'm going to be just like her when I grow up."

"Oh," I said, "well, sometimes a coincidence is just a coincidence."

"Who said that?" she said.

"Me, just then."

"Oh." She sounded disappointed. "I thought it might have been Percy Jackson or Ruby Redfort."

"Well, I bet they *wished* they'd said it," I said. "It's an excellent observation."

"Maybe," she said, not sounding very convinced.

Boy, this kid was a tough nut. Maybe the toughest nut I'd ever encountered. She was definitely a macadamia.

### Note to you

Macadamias are the hardest nuts in the world. If you're hungry and in a hurry, don't try to crack a macadamia. Eat peanuts or pistachios instead.

But even tough nuts have soft spots. You just need to look around the edges.

"Okay," I said, "what did she look like?"

"She was wearing a long leather coat and a hat."

"So, you couldn't see her face?"

"No," she said. "I was writing down her description in my notebook and when I leaned forward to get a better look at her, I dropped the notebook out the window. She picked it up, tore out the page, stomped on it, and walked away. I think my notebook's still in the gutter."

**The Hero's Handbook**
**Top Tip 42:** Try to keep body bits inside windows.

I looked at the empty column for CLUES in the Hero Hotline Help Ledger. "So you nearly had a clue and then you didn't," I said.

## Note to you

This kid is clueless.

"Yes," she said. "I mean no. But there's more."
"Good," I said. "More is good."

## Note to you

But most is better.

I looked at Ellie who was still monitoring the tracker. She shook her head. *Keep going,* she mouthed.

"What else?" I said.

"It was the next day when I found it," she said.

"Found what?" I said.

"What I think she wants," she said. "She's waiting for me to make a move."

"What kind of move?" I said.

"I don't know," she said. "That's why I'm calling you."

Ellie said I had an excellent imagination and a tendency to be dramatic but this kid was off the drama scale. She'd definitely been reading too many

Penelope Fuggletons. This current line of inquiry was more like a circle. I was back where I started. I decided to ask something easy.

"What's your name?" I said.

"Marley," she said. "Marley Hart."

"Okay, Marley," I said, "I'll need your address, please, so we can–"

There was a crash and a bang on the other end of the phone.

"Marley," I said, "are you still there? Hello?"

The flat tone of the phone filled my ears. The line was dead.

I looked at Ellie and shook my head.

But Ellie smiled. "It's okay," she said. "I got a fix on the call. I know where she is."

## Chapter Three

# Meeting Marley

"THIS IS IT," said Ellie, as she looked up from Google Maps. "Twenty-four Tavistock Avenue."

We stared at the white three-story row house in front of us. The front door was wide and grand, and enormous bay windows with velvet curtains, tied with swishy sashes, looked out onto the street. Neatly trimmed bushes on either side guarded the steps up to the front door, and rose bushes bloomed in between them.

"This would have been a fancy part of town in the old days," said Ellie, checking out the street, which was still quiet in the early morning. An elderly woman was walking with a toddler, and a man in a dark-blue suit and a leather briefcase was striding with purpose.

Ellie and I had left HoMe at dawn and caught

a cab from the airport straight here.

"It's shabby chic now," said Ellie. "They don't make places this spacious anymore."

"Marley was probably looking out one of those windows," I said and pointed to the tall windows on the third story of the house. "She said she could see most of the street from there."

We turned as the quick toot of a horn sounded and a black Audi pulled up beside us. Alex and his dad waved, parked the car and climbed out.

We had spoken to them last night and filled them in on Marley's call.

It had only been two days since we'd seen them at HoMe but Alex looked even taller, if that was anatomically possible.

He saw me assessing the length from his head to his toes.

"Yeah, I know," he said. "I had growing pains overnight."

*Growing pains!* I sighed. He was so lucky. I'd read about growing pains but I didn't think I was ever going to have them.

"Oh, well," I said, trying not to be alarmed at the growing distance between us. "You can still see the top and I can still see the bottom. We've just got even more of the world covered now."

Alex smiled.

Timothy Fischer looked at his watch. "Sorry, everyone, but I've got to dash into the city for a meeting at the Super Sleuth Association. They've got a few questions about the report I've just filed on my last assignment."

## Note to you
His last assignment was to find my parents.
Status: ongoing.

He smiled at Ellie. "Paper pushers," he said. "Anything inconclusive fills them with horror."

Ellie laughed and smiled at Timothy Fischer. He smiled back even more. I looked at Ellie smiling at Timothy Fischer smiling at Ellie. There was a lot of smiling going on.

## Note to you
It takes more muscles to smile than it does to frown so smile often for a great workout.

They were enclosed in a bubble of smiles.

Alex had noticed it too. He looked from his dad to Ellie and then back to his dad. He tapped on the bubble.

"Ah, Dad," he said. "You'd better get going. You'll be late."

"Hmmm," said Timothy Fischer, his smile getting wider and wider. He was going for the workout of workouts.

"DAD!" said Alex.

Timothy Fischer looked startled. "There's no need to shout, Alex," he said. "I'm right here."

He walked around to the driver's side of the car and then hesitated. "Actually, Ellie," he said as he opened the door, "I may need an independent witness to corroborate my report. Someone who was at the heart of the incident."

"Oh, I'd love to come," said Ellie, running down the steps to the Audi. "I mean, of course, I'm happy to help in any way I can. Is that okay with you, Henrie?"

"Sure," I said. "Alex and I can take things from here."

Alex nodded.

"And while I'm in the city," said Ellie, giving me a quick hug goodbye, "I'll pop into the lawyer F.C. Gerrard told us about."

F.C. Gerrard, HoMe's lawyer, thought this city lawyer might have more up-to-date information about my mum and dad because the address she had for them was nearly twelve years old. *Twelve years!* If a lot could happen in three days since meeting Albert Abernathy and standing outside 24 Tavistock Avenue, imagine how much could happen in twelve years?

I thought of all the lives Mum and Dad had had already and were still having:

**With HoMe.**

**Without HoMe.**

**With me** (a Very Short Life).

**Without me** (a Very Long Life because it was all of my life, except for the quickest of hellos in the hospital).

Even if we did find each other, through all the moments and milestones that separated us, would we ever put together the missing pieces between us? They could fill a huge hall of longing.

Ellie gave me a jigsaw of the sky once. It had four thousand pieces and they were all blue with an occasional whisper of a cloud, blowing in from the side. I laid out all the pieces carefully on the kitchen table and I felt hope sink.

Like now.

Ellie jumped in the car and waved. We watched as the Audi pulled out and drove off down the street. Ellie was laughing at something Alex's dad had said.

"That was weird," I said.

"Yeah, Dad's been weird since we got home," said Alex. "Kind of fidgety and excited. This morning, he leaped out of bed yelling BEAUTIFUL DAY as soon as the alarm went off. He *never* leaps out of bed yelling BEAUTIFUL DAY. He says it's unnatural to rise *and* shine. He says it puts too much pressure on getting up."

"Who knows what goes on in grown-ups' heads," I said. "The more I meet, the more confusing they are." I looked up at the front door of 24 Tavistock Avenue. "Maybe *I* should knock on the door. If there's a grown-up inside, they won't suspect a short kid of subterfuge. Tall kids look more suspicious, like they're only pretending to be kids."

"Well, okay, I guess," said Alex. "I'll hide behind that bush." He pointed to the third one on the left.

I waited for him to crouch into position and then walked up the steps to the front door. There was a buzzer to the right of the door handle and I pushed it. I could hear it ringing inside – an old-fashioned *ding dong* – and footsteps approaching.

I tried to slow my heart so I could speak normally. Nerves love messing with your voice. My drama teacher said so.

### Note to you
I know my nerves are mine but they don't seem to like me very much.

The door opened.

A girl in jeans and boots with sleek, straight, shoulder-length hair and headphones looked at me.

My hair envy was immediate.

I'd always wanted sleek, straight, shoulder-length hair.

Mine was wavy and bobbed up at unexpected angles. Like a ship in a storm.

I'd always thought someone else had gotten the hair that should have been mine, and now I knew who.

### Her.

Ellie said we had to be thankful for what we got even if it was the exact opposite of what we wanted.

I hoped life wasn't going to be like this all the time.

The girl with my hair smiled at me.

She was tapping her foot in time to the music. It sounded strangled, like it was coming out of tin cans.

"Hello," I said.

"What?" she shouted.

I pointed to her headphones. "Whoops, sorry," she said, taking them off. "I forget they're there most of the time."

"Is Marley home?" I said. "We're … um … at … um … school together."

"Well, that's funny," said the girl, frowning.

"What's funny?" I said.

"Marley hasn't started school yet," she said.

"Oh, well … I mean …" I said, trying to think faster than my words, "… we're *going* to be at school together. I've just moved here," I said. "From … from … Iceland."

"Iceland?" she said.

"Yes, Iceland," I said. "It's really cold there and I'm still thawing out so sometimes my words sound frozen together."

## The Hero's Handbook
**Top Tip 29:** Work out what you're going to say before you say it. Words can trip and tickle.

The girl looked at me. She had an *"I-don't-believe-a-word-of-what-you've-just-said"* look on her face.

I knew that look because Ellie gets it when I'm trying to tell her a tall story (although, in my case it was more of a short story).

### Note to you
A short story is easier to believe than a tall story. It doesn't have to travel as far.

I had to change the subject as fast as I could.

"Are you Marley's ... sister?" I said.

"No, I'm Poppy," she said. "Her kidsitter. Who are you?"

"I'm Henrie," I said.

"Are you here all by yourself, Henrie?" said Poppy, looking up and down the street. "You look a bit young to be out on your own."

"It's only because I'm short for my age," I said. "I'm tall on the inside."

Poppy laughed. "You sound like Marley. She's always saying strange stuff like that. But you didn't answer my question."

"My aunt's with me," I said. "She's parking the car." I waved vaguely down the street. "We're going for coffee but I just wanted to say hello to Marley first. I don't know any kids in my class yet. Mrs. ... Lepanski ... from ..." I looked across the street at the houses opposite, "from ... a few doors down said Marley was going to be at the same school as me."

### Note to you

This is not really fibbing. It's more like creative writing. You know. The stuff you do at school.

41

"Well, I'll tell Marley you stopped by," said Poppy. "She's busy at the moment. What did you say your name was again?"

"Henrie," I said. "Henrie Melchior."

"Well, nice to meet you, Henrie," she said, closing the door in my face.

I walked back down the steps.

Alex poked his head out from behind the bush. He raised his eyebrow in a question.

"It's okay," I said. "She's going to leave the house soon."

"How do you know?" he said.

"She had a shopping list in her hand and she put a supermarket bag down by the door when she opened it."

"Top observation," said Alex.

I nodded. He was right.

Just as I'd predicted with my **top observation,** we didn't have to wait long.

Ten minutes later Poppy skipped down the front steps, yelling behind her, "Won't be long, Marley. Don't answer the door while I'm gone. There are some strange people about."

I looked at Alex. She didn't mean me, did she?

We watched Poppy walk to the end of the street, swinging her shopping bag in time to the music

42

in her head. As soon as she turned the corner, Alex and I raced up the steps to the front door of 24 Tavistock Avenue.

"Ready?" I said.

Alex nodded and rang the doorbell.

After what seemed like a long time, the mail slot in the door opened.

A pair of brown eyes peered through it.

I bent down to talk to them.

"Marley?" I said. "Is that you?"

"Maybe," said the squeaky voice I had heard on the Hero Hotline. "Who wants to know?"

"Me," I said. "Henrie. From HoMe. I talked to you on the phone."

"How do I know you're who you say you are?" she said. "I'm not allowed to open the door to strangers."

"Ask me a question," I said. "Something only I'd know because I was the one talking to you."

"Okay," she said. "Who was the stranger *you* said you didn't know you could trust?"

Alex was standing right behind me so I whispered my words into the slot. "Alex Fischer."

But Alex heard me anyway. And jabbed me in the ribs. *Ouch!*

I glared at him. He glared at me.

"Well, it's true," I said, turning to him and rubbing

43

my ribs. "You suddenly turned up outside my house with a skateboard and heaps of money and available for an adventure. *That's* not normal."

"But I explained all that," said Alex.

"Eventually," I said.

"*And* I said I was sorry for not telling you," he said.

"It was a sorry situation, all right," I said.

"Who are you talking to?" said Marley.

"Alex Fischer," I said.

"I told you to come alone," she said.

"No, you didn't," I said.

"Well, I meant to say that," said Marley. "They always say that in the movies."

"Well, it wouldn't have mattered if you'd said that, anyway," I said. "Where I go Alex Fischer goes."

"Yeah," said Alex, bending down to talk to the slot. "Henrie and me, we're a team."

"Well, okay, I guess," said Marley, slowly. "I'm going to open the door. But you'd better be who you say you are. I've got a Great Dane next to me and he hasn't had breakfast."

I'd seen a Great Dane on TV once. It was taller than me. Maybe even taller than Alex Fischer. I stepped back behind him. He had more hope of eyeballing a Great Dane than I did.

The door began to open.

# Chapter Four

# A Girl, a Great-Aunt, a Mystery

**A GIRL IN** a wheelchair was in front of us. Her long black hair was tied back in a ponytail, and she was wearing a red dress dotted with white fish.

Her left leg was in plaster up to her thigh and a curly poodle was fast asleep on her lap. Maybe it was dreaming of being a Great Dane. It looked as far from ferocious as it could possibly be.

I stepped forward. "Marley?" I said.

"Maybe," she said. She looked from Alex to me and back again. "Show me some credentials."

*Credentials?*

"Well," I said, "I can't curl my tongue but I can wiggle my ears."

Marley frowned.

"I don't think she means those kind of credentials," said Alex.

"Who are *you*, anyway?" said Marley, turning to stare at Alex. She looked at him from top to toe. It took her a long time to travel the whole distance.

"I'm Henrie's Hero Advisor," said Alex.

"Well, Hero Advisor," said Marley, "I don't think you're doing a very good job."

Alex blushed.

47

"In fact," she said, "*I'd* advise *you* to advise your hero to get a better pitch together. She hasn't been much like a hero so far."

"I'm right here, you know," I said. "And I'd advise *you* to stop being such a smarty-pants."

Marley grinned. "Fair enough," she said. "I like your attitude."

"Anyway," I said, "how many heroes have you met?"

"Just you," she said.

I smiled on the inside. *Good. She doesn't know this is my first Hero Hunt.*

"It's just that I expected you to be more like Penelope Fuggleton," she said.

"Who's Penelope Fuggleton?" said Alex.

"Only the most famous kid detective in the history of kid detectives," said Marley. "Don't you know anything?"

"We're too busy solving real crimes to read kids' stories," I said.

Marley smirked. I think she could see right through me. And way beyond.

"*And* attending meetings of the Super Sleuth Association," I added.

"Really?" she said. Now I had her attention. And it wasn't really a lie. It was a fib en route to the truth. Alex's dad said they had a program for the Under 14s and he was going to nominate me at the next meeting.

Then I remembered that Marley was a macadamia. I needed to find her soft spot.

"What happened to you?" I said, looking at her leg.

"I fell off my scooter and fractured my tibia in two places," she said, pointing to her plaster. Alex and I looked at it too. Someone had written: YOU'RE BLUFFING in blue marker on it.

"My dad," she said, tapping the cast. "He thinks he's funny. He's always laughing at his own jokes. Mum says we have to humor him. Dad says he humer-us too."

## Note to you
This is a not-very-good pun.

## Another note to you
The humerus is the funny bone but the funny bone isn't a bone at all. It's a nerve. It's got a nerve, all right — posing as a bone.

*Marley has very punny parents*, I thought. I wondered if my mum and dad were punny? I hoped they were. Puns were funny and made me laugh. Ellie was always laughing so maybe it ran in Mum's side of the family?

I didn't know if Dad was a laugher but the Melchiors I had met so far didn't laugh much (except when Carter locked me in the old, pitch-black factory quarters, but his laugh was evil, low and slow. You know the kind I mean. There are heaps on YouTube. Especially around Halloween).

"Cool cast," said Alex.

"Do you want to see my X-ray?" said Marley, wheeling herself across to the cupboard against the wall.

"Yeah, that'd be great," I said, stepping into the hall. I couldn't wait to break a bone. I loved looking at X-rays. The bones always looked startled. As if they'd been interrupted in the middle of a bone party and someone had yelled FREEZE.

Mrs. Petrie told us all about bones in biology last term. She even brought a skeleton to school.

"Did you pack it in a suitcase?" said Will Distemper.

"Of course not," said Mrs. Petrie, looking horrified. "That's no way to treat a skeleton. Leroy sat next to me on the bus.

"People did look at me strangely," said Mrs. Petrie, "and I heard someone mutter they were going to call the police." She placed her hand on Leroy's head. He smiled. "But there's no need to be ashamed of your bones, children. Bones are beautiful."

Mrs. Petrie's father had been a doctor and he'd inherited Leroy from his father, so Leroy had been the family skeleton in the closet for years.

Leroy hung on the back of our classroom door for a month while we worked our way up and down his body. He always looked cheerful, even when he was just hanging around. But, one day, Mrs. Petrie said it was time to take Leroy home. We waved goodbye to Mrs. Petrie and Leroy as they caught the train. (Mrs. Petrie wanted to give Leroy a different public transportation experience.)

### Note to you

We have 270 bones when we're born but by the time we grow up we've only got 206 bones.

Q: Where do those bones go?

A: To find some body.

"Thanks but maybe later," said Alex, interrupting my memory of Leroy. "We'd better start following up some leads."

I frowned at him. He was right but I wish I'd said we had to start "following up some leads." Those words sounded very professional.

Marley looked impressed too.

"Yes," I said, "we need to follow up some leads."

Marley didn't look as impressed when I said it. I guess because she'd heard the words before.

I took out my notebook.

"Tell us in your own words what happened," I said, pen poised like a real-life hero.

"Well, they would be my words," said Marley. "They couldn't be anyone else's words."

Alex laughed. "She's got you there, Henrie."

I frowned. This was not going the way I'd planned. "Do you want our help or not, Marley? I've got more important things to do," (*like find my parents*), "if you don't."

"Sorry," said Marley. "Mum says I should listen more and speak less so people don't think I'm a know-it-all. I know nobody likes a know-it-all, but I haven't had anyone to listen to for ages so I'm a bit rusty. We've just moved here and I don't know anyone and then I broke my leg so I've been stuck inside."

"What about Poppy?" I said.

"She's a teenager," said Marley. "I can't listen to her because *she* listens to music all day and sighs every time I ask her something."

"Start from the beginning," said Alex. "Tell us

53

everything that happened. Don't worry about making sense of it. That's Henrie's job. She's great at doing that."

Marley looked at me like she didn't believe Alex but she started anyway.

"So, yesterday, Mum and I were unpacking boxes," said Marley. "I was unwrapping the newspaper around Great-Aunt Agnes's Chinese porcelain tea set and I saw that she'd underlined an ad in the paper. I kept it. Look."

Marley pulled out a torn section of newspaper from her pocket.

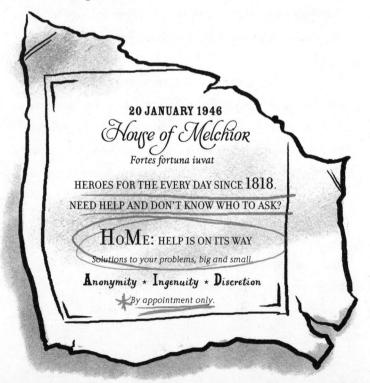

**20 JANUARY 1946**

*House of Melchior*

*Fortes fortuna iuvat*

HEROES FOR THE EVERY DAY SINCE 1818.

NEED HELP AND DON'T KNOW WHO TO ASK?

HoMe: HELP IS ON ITS WAY

*Solutions to your problems, big and small.*

**A**nonymity ★ **I**ngenuity ★ **D**iscretion

*By appointment only.*

"I asked Mum why Great-Aunt Agnes would have underlined this but she didn't know. I thought it was curious and might be important so I kept it. I could smell a mystery."

"It was probably the newspaper," I said, wrinkling my nose, and handing the yellowed, crusty piece of paper to Alex. The past was so smelly.

"What did your aunt do?" I said.

"She was an archaeologist," said Marley. She whizzed her wheelchair around and wheeled herself over to the Mac sitting on the big oak desk in the corner.

She keyed in Agnes Hart and Wikipedia popped up.

### Agnes Hart, archaeologist and explorer: 1895–1980

After graduating with First Class Honours in History and Classics from Cambridge University, Miss Hart became a pioneer in a field not known for its female exponents. At a time when most young women were pursuing marriage and motherhood with great gusto, Miss Hart was rolling up her sleeves and digging in the dirt. After several significant archaeological finds in the Valley of the Queens in Egypt, she met the renowned Egyptologist Howard Carter. He persuaded her to join his team in the Valley of the Kings, searching for the undiscovered tomb of the boy pharaoh Tutankhamen. When World War I broke out, Miss Hart joined the WRENS and served in France. She returned to the Valley of the Kings after the war, to resume the dig with Howard Carter and his team, but departed the site the day of the most significant discovery in the history of Egyptology – a discovery that would have enshrined her name in the history books. Miss Hart retired from society and became a recluse. Little is known about her subsequent life. She is buried at Stepton Village.

Alex and Marley were looking at me expectantly. "Interesting," I said, writing in my notebook. "So, first question: Why did Agnes depart the site so abruptly? On the day they discovered Tutankhamen's tomb?"

"Mum says Great-Aunt Agnes never talked about it," said Marley. "But she always got the feeling there was some big mystery around it. Something that Great-Aunt Agnes never got over."

"Hmm," I said, checking out the photo of Agnes's gravestone that was at the bottom of the entry. There was a small bunch of dried rosemary in a jar propped up next to it. Ellie had said that rosemary was for remembrance. I wonder who'd put it there?

"What does *Veritas Nunquam Perit* mean?" said Alex, pointing to the words.

"'*The truth never perishes,*'" said Marley.

"You know Latin?" asked Alex, sounding impressed.

"No, Mum does," said Marley. "She said Great-Aunt Agnes asked for that to be inscribed on her tombstone."

"Aha," I said.

"Aha what?" said Marley.

"Don't you see?" I said.

"See what?" said Marley.

"It's obvious," I said. "Your aunt contacted HoMe for help and then left a message on her gravestone about truth never dying."

"So?" said Marley.

"So, she died before the truth about something could be uncovered," I said. My thoughts were racing ahead of me, shouting as they fled:

**Catch us. Catch us. Hurry up. Hurry up.**

Dots were flinging themselves about on the page in my notebook. I tried to calm them down but dots that weren't connected had minds of their own.

"Look at the pictures under the inscription," I said.

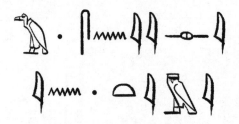

"Egyptian hieroglyphics," said Alex. "Probably just decoration."

"But what if they aren't just for decoration?" I said.

"What do you mean?" said Marley.

"What if there's a message in them?"

"A message?" said Marley.

"A message for who?" said Alex.

"Actually, it's 'for whom,'" I said. Mr. Tribble was very particular about our whos and whoms.

"You mean, a message from the grave," said Marley, with eyes wide open.

"Exactly," I said.

We looked up the hieroglyphic alphabet online.

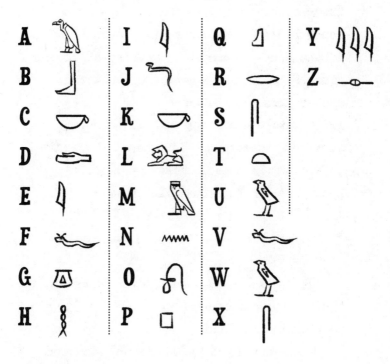

## Note to you

Can you work out the clue?

Your answer: _____

I looked at the words the hieroglyphs had spelled out:

**A sneeze in time**

"It doesn't sound very Egyptian," said Marley. "What does it mean?"

"I don't know," I said.

## The Hero's Handbook

**Top Tip 31:** Sometimes a clue doesn't look like a clue. It might be wearing a wig and glasses. Or a false nose and moustache. Look beyond what you see.

**PS** We advise you not to pull the aforementioned moustache until you have irrefutable proof that it's false.

**Examples of irrefutable proof:**

* It wobbles in the wind.
* It dangles at a suspicious angle.

"Okay," I said, "let's break it down. So it's usually 'a stitch in time saves nine.'"

"What is?" said Marley.

"The saying," I said. "A stitch in time saves nine."

"Never heard of it," said Marley. I could tell by the way she said this she thought I had no idea what I was talking about.

**Note to you**
I bet you know the way she said it. As if she was
**puffing** the words in my face.

Penelope Fuggleton had set high hero standards.
They were so towering I couldn't even see them.

"But how does the sneeze fit in?" said Alex.

"Maybe it's a hieroglyphic typo?" said Marley.
"They both have six letters."

"I can't imagine an Egyptian scribe making that kind
of typo though," I said. "The words might start with the
same letter but they're not like each other at all."

"Unless the person sneezed while writing stitch
and wrote sneeze instead?" said Marley.

"Dad pulled a stitch when he sneezed," said Alex.

"My uncle Arthur blew his wife across the room
with *his* sneeze," said Marley.

**Note to you**
Never snort at the power of a sneeze.

I closed my eyes and tried to get sneezes and
stitches to form some kind of pattern in my head.

*Nope.*
*Nothing.*

61

When I opened my eyes, Alex and Marley were staring at me, waiting for me to say something hero-y. "I've got a feeling Agnes is telling us to look for stitches *and* sneezes," I said slowly.

**The Hero's Handbook**
Top Tip 52: Follow your feeling. Guts are good. (Except when they're greedy.)

"Of course," said Alex. "That makes so much sense. NOT."

I glared at him.

I turned to Marley. "Do you have anything of Agnes's with stitches?"

"Actually," said Marley, after thinking for a moment. "We've got her embroidery box. Mum said Agnes left it to her in her will. She thought it was a strange thing to leave and was hoping for one of Agnes's first editions but Cousin Basil got those. But Mum said if the embroidery box was precious to Agnes then it was precious to her."

"Good," I said. "If Agnes mentioned it in her will then it's got to be important. Where is it?"

"Stuffed at the back of the closet in the guest bedroom," said Marley. "Behind Dad's bowling bag and cricket pads."

"I can get it," said Alex, "if you show me where it is."

"Follow me," said Marley, leading Alex into the downstairs bedroom.

They were back a couple of minutes later with an embroidery box sitting in Marley's lap.

She put it on the table and we rummaged through it, taking out all the hoops, needles, threads, fabric and a seam ripper.

"Mum was going to teach me embroidery," said Marley, holding a hoop with an embroidered house and garden, "but she's away for work so often we haven't got around to it yet."

I looked at Marley. Her words sounded a little lonely. She had a mum and a dad but they were Missing in Action too. Like mine. At least *she* knew where they were. I thought of Ellie. She should have seen the city lawyer by now. She might be holding

Mum and Dad's address in her hand. I closed my eyes and wished as hard as I could that she was. I wanted to believe that wishing could make things come true. I tried it last year for my birthday. But I didn't get a pony. Or a dog. My wish must have gotten mixed up with someone else's. That must happen all the time with wishes firing here, there and everywhere. Like shooting stars. Or blazing comets. Burning up the night sky.

"Wait a minute," I said, my eye spying a little embroidery pocket, tucked in the corner of the box. "It's a hankie holder. Ellie had one like this from her grandmother. They were big in the Old Days. And a hankie has sneezes." I opened it with excitement as Marley and Alex crowded close.

"Oh," said Marley, as I pulled out three lace hankies. "It's full of hankies."

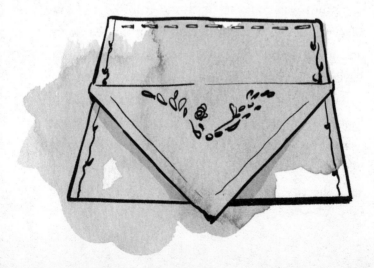

"So we found the sneeze but not the stitch," said Alex.

I took out each dainty hankie and looked at it closely. I put the hankie holder on the table in front of us and then turned it upside down and inside out.

Still nothing. We were all sneezed out.

Or were we?

I leaned forward in my chair as one thought clambered on top of all the others, waving a flag at me, trying to get my attention. Maybe there was something. *Saves nine.*

"Look," I said. "At the top of the hankie holder."

"There are stitches," said Marley.

"How many?" I said.

"123456789," said Marley, in a rush.

"Hand me the seam ripper," I said, like a surgeon in a heart operation asking for a scalpel.

I unpicked the stitches as Alex and Marley huddled in even closer.

As the last stitch came away, we all gasped. There was a secret sleeve in the hankie holder. And folded up inside were a couple of pieces of paper. And a tiny key with a number at the top of it: **307**.

My hand shook as I unfolded the lined pages, and laid them out in front of us on the table.

"These must be from Agnes's diary," I said.

"Agnes isn't here to tell us what happened but her diary might. And we've got a key for something."

"Keys open secrets," said Marley with wide eyes.

**We had found Clue No. 1.**

# Chapter Five

# Clues News

**WE LOOKED AT** the diary entries. There were two in total. Two that Agnes must be saying were the most important ones. Why else would she have kept them secret like this? Or was she hiding them from someone?

My heart was thudding. We were just like archaeologists and this banging on my ribs was what it felt like to discover something that had been lying unseen, for years and years. Waiting for someone to find it and give it a voice.

I read the first sheet of paper out loud.

*28 June 1946*
*I have found someone to help me uncover the truth.*
*My truth. For how I yearn to be free of suspicion.*
*I have let it cast too long a shadow over my life.*

*An accusation is as damaging as a guilty verdict. My life has been blighted by this falsehood.*

*PS I am amused his name means "King." If I believed in a divine power, I would believe that this is a sign. We shall reveal the truth. Together.*

"1946," I said, pointing to the date at the top of the entry. "The same year she circled the ad for HoMe."

"Someone whose name means 'King,'" Alex said. "What does that mean?"

Marley shook her head. "I don't know. It doesn't mean anything to me." She turned to me. "But that's why you're here."

She smiled at me for the first time and I knew why.

She was starting to trust me.

She was beginning to believe I knew what I was doing.

## The Hero's Handbook
**Top Tip 71:** Making other people think you know what you're doing is more important sometimes than actually knowing what you are doing.

**Psst.** Between you and me, I didn't really know what I was doing but I was doing my best and Ellie said that was the main thing.

I smiled back as confidently as I could.

**Note to you**

For a confident smile: stretch your mouth wide + show lots of teeth. Practice in the mirror until you get it right.

"What about the other page?" said Alex.

I looked at the second sheet of paper but it was ripped all the way up the middle and only had four words on it.

## Need to prove my—

"Need to prove my what?" said Marley.

"I don't know," I said.

Agnes had wanted someone to read these entries. She had left us a key to something. But what? I turned the tiny key around in my hand. It was too small to be a house key. Maybe it was the key to her diary? I once had a diary that had a lock.

We had found our first clue but it was a clue with

questions, leaping at us from every angle. So many questions tumbling through my head and not an answer in sight.

Not yet, anyway.

"Something doesn't smell right," I said. Then I had a thought. "Where's that piece of newspaper Agnes used to wrap the porcelain?"

"In the trash," said Alex.

"What's it doing in the trash?" I said.

"I put it there," said Alex. "We didn't need it anymore."

"Don't we?" I said. "What if we've missed something vitally important?"

"Have we?" said Alex.

"If you get the newspaper we can find out," I said.

"Me?" said Alex. "Why me?"

"Because it's a dirty job," I said, "and someone's got to do it. Marley can't walk, and I'm thinking. I can't mastermind a trash extraction *and* think."

"But that trash stinks," said Alex.

"Poppy forgot to put it out last night," said Marley.

"Great," said Alex. "Who's got a nose peg?"

Marley and I shook our heads.

I wrote a *PS* in my notebook:

Keep nose pegs close at all times.

## The Hero's Handbook

**Top Tip 8:** Trash cans ooze with details. They also ooze with detritus. A hero must deduce which is which. PS They can smell the same.

**Top Tip 8a:** Wear gloves. And possibly a nose peg.
Trash is stinky.
Details can be stinky too.

**Top Tip 8b:** However repugnant these smells may be, do not allow your nostrils to think for you.

Alex stomped off to the trash can.

"Do you think the girl was after the newspaper?" said Marley.

"Maybe," I said. "Or maybe not."

Alex came back a few minutes later. He'd found some rubber gloves in the kitchen and was holding the piece of newspaper out in front of him. It had chicken curry stains down one side.

He held it out to me. "What?" I said. "I'm not going to touch it."

"Me neither," said Marley.

Alex sighed and flattened it out on the table.

We inspected it (at a distance) from top to bottom.

There were articles about Petrol Tickets and an RAAF man who had disappeared again, and ads for Bath Powder and Wrinkle Cream for Mature Skin. It all looked suspiciously unsuspicious ... until I saw three small words written next to an ad for nasal hair removal.

"Have you got a magnifying glass, please, Marley?" I said.

Marley grabbed one from the desk.

"Museum of Antiquities," I said.

"That's in the city," said Alex. "You know, that big gray old building that backs onto the park."

"Oh, yeah," said Marley. "Dad said it's full of Egyptian treasures."

"Okay, good," I said. "Looks like we're going to the Museum of Antiquities to find out what was important to Agnes there."

"Okay but first, stay right there," said Marley, wheeling herself toward the door. "Don't say or do anything. I don't want to miss any new thoughts." She wheeled herself into the hall and we heard her throwing things on the floor.

"You know," said Alex, in a quiet voice while we waited, "you and Marley are a bit alike."

I looked at him in horror – too shocked to answer.

"In fact," he said, "have you noticed your initials are mirror images of each other?"

"We are nothing alike," I said, my words rushing back to me. "Marley's a bossy smarty-pants."

Alex smirked.

"What?" I said. "I'm not a bossy smarty-pants!" Then I had a terrible thought. *Am I?*

Marley appeared at the door before Alex could reply but he was still smirking so I guess he didn't need to. She had two walkie-talkies in her lap.

"If we're going on a mission we need mission equipment," she said. "Penelope Fuggleton said spies need spy stuff." She handed a walkie-talkie to me and kept one for herself. "These might be handy. Especially if we're separated during a dramatic chase. I guess because you're a hero you've used one before?"

"Of course," I said. "Heroes learn walkie-talkie talk before our ABCs."

**Note to you**
**Shhh.** I know you know this doesn't even have a whiff of truth about it because I've been a hero for about five minutes.

## Walkie-Talkie Talk

| | |
|---|---|
| **Do you copy?** | Can you hear me? |
| **Copy that** | I can hear you |
| **Roger that** | Message received |
| **Affirmative** | Yes |
| **Negative** | No |
| **What's your 20?** | Where are you? |
| **Eyes on** | I can see them |
| **Eyes off** | I've lost them |

"And we have to have code names," said Marley. "We can't use our real names. That would blow our cover."

"I'll be GREENPEA," I said. I loved peas. I could eat them morning, noon and night. Especially mashed ones. On toast.

"I'll be TIBS," said Marley. "On account of my tibia."

We waited for Alex. "Um," he said, "I'll be …" He paused and scratched his head. His thought was obviously stuck. But we were in a hurry. I'd have to think for him.

"How about FISHFACE?" I said.

"Excellent," said Marley.

"Well, it's not as good as GREENPEA or TIBS," said Alex, screwing up his nose.

"Well, those names are already taken," I said.

Marley and I looked at each other. It was obvious: Alex had never had a code name before.

"I'll be … MOVE IT MOVE IT," said Alex.

"Hmm," I said. "Dramatic. But too long. How about we shorten it to … MIMI."

### Note to you

MIMI is an acronym for MOVE IT MOVE IT.

Make up as many mission acronyms as you can today.

"Okay, good," said Alex, nodding. "Yeah. I like MIMI."

"Let's try them out," I said. "Alex and I'll go upstairs and you stay down here, Marley."

"Roger that, GREENPEA," said Marley.

I raised my eyebrow at Alex and we left TIBS downstairs in trying-out-walkie-talkie position.

Alex and I had just gotten to the top of the stairs when the walkie-talkie crackled.

"Do you copy, GREENPEA?" said Marley, in a tiny voice.

"Copy that, TIBS," I said, "but only just. Why are you whispering?"

"Eyes on," she said.

"What?" I said.

"There's somebody at the door. I think it's her."

"Who?" I said.

"The girl who was following me."

"Roger that," I said. "We're coming."

Alex and I hurtled down the stairs, two at a time.

Halfway down, Marley crackled through the walkie-talkie. "She's trying to get in." Then she screamed.

Alex and I arrived on the ground floor as the door was opening. A girl in a long black leather coat was trying to *swish* through the door as Marley blocked it with her wheelchair.

The girl was about to push Marley out of the way when she saw us. She tried to back out of the door but Marley snagged some of her coat in the wheels of her chair. The girl was stuck. They pulled and tugged with each other.

With a furious final yank and a loud rip, the girl freed herself from the wheels, pushed Marley out of the way, ran out the door and slammed it behind her.

Alex tore after her. At the bottom of the steps, he tried to grab her but she shook him off and kept running. She was already disappearing down the end of the street by the time I caught up to Alex.

She was the fastest crook I'd ever encountered.

### Note to you

She was a Champion Sprinter Crook. There's probably a special Olympics for Crooks where they compete in events like the Bag Snatcher 100 meters, the Cat Burglar Pole Vault and the Pickpocket Hurdles.

"She got away," I said, bending over and puffing.

"But she left something behind," said Alex. He was poking around in the gutter with a stick. It had rained overnight and a bunch of leaves were clogging the drain. That was the only reason whatever it was hadn't sailed off down the drain already, surfing the stormwaters to be spewed out into the sea. Funny how luck can beam in from above like a spotlight and point you in the right direction at the right time. "I think it fell out of her pocket," he said, plucking a card from the leaves. "Part of the pocket must have ripped when Marley caught it in her wheels." He handed the card to me. It was soggy around the edges and covered in small bits of drain debris, but we could still read it.

ANTIQUARIAN BOOK COLLECTOR

FREDERIC FORTESCUE

52 BLEACHLEY BOULEVARD

MILLBROOK

I smiled at Alex.

**We'd just found Clue No. 2.**

## The Art of Following a Clue, or a Person of Interest

The aim of sleuthing is to remain inconspicuous, which is a ridiculously long word for something that means not attracting attention. A five-syllable word has already attracted far more attention than it should. In more succinct and approachable words: **blend in, not out.**

**Top Tip 1:** Consider the color of the day and dress accordingly. If the day is gray and gloomy, dress in subdued colors, such as brown, or beige. A black umbrella is an excellent accessory. If it rains, you will become part of a pattern of black umbrellas, wending along the street.

If the day is sunny and bright, dress in yellow, orange or red to match the sartorial mood of the people around you. Beige and/or black on a sunny day scream: LOOK AT ME.

**Top Tip 2:** Carry a phone, book or newspaper, the latter of which can be very handy to pull up in front of your whole face. Appear thoroughly engrossed in your phone, book or newspaper.

Of course, the opposite is actually true. Your eyes are those of an eagle, keenly observing every interaction, every quick movement that may signal information has been exchanged; every tilt of the head suggesting **Person of Interest at 4 o'clock**. Nonverbal communication is the most effective tool at your disposal. Use it as often as possible. Convey much with little.

**Top Tip 3:** Wearing a hero disguise, such as a wig and dark glasses, is also an option. However, consider your choices carefully. You must be able to see clearly, and only movie stars wear dark glasses inside. You are not a movie star. You are not even a movie star in training. You are a hero in training. Stay focused.

PS High, gusty winds play havoc with hair and are especially catastrophic to wig-wearing operatives. Consult the Beaufort Scale for wind force before leaving the house.

# How to spot being spotted

Suspicion is alert and vigilant. A glance held a nanosecond too long is all it takes to raise its hackles. Be prepared to walk in the opposite direction if you think you have been spotted. Avoid becoming the suspect of the suspect. It is far better to double back, or slip down a side street, than to double down with inaction and risk exposure.

To throw the suspect off the scent, greet a stranger warmly and ask them for directions, or the time. Strangers will be cordial for at least 30 seconds before becoming irritated by your intrusion. This is usually long enough to convey the illusion of conversation between two friends and allay the suspect's suspicion.

# Chapter Six

# Pea Man

**WE CAUGHT THE** train to Poole Street Station and pushed Marley along the sidewalk. She was pretty good at getting around corners and just needed an extra push when the street was steeper. It was nearly midday by now and people from nearby offices were spilling onto the streets, seeking food or friends.

We'd done the best of three in rock, paper, scissors to decide whether to check out Frederic Fortescue or the Museum of Antiquities first. Frederic Fortescue had been scissors to Marley's paper.

Sometimes in the hero business, you have to choose between clues – like choosing to go in one direction rather than another. You don't know it's wrong until it's not right.

**The Hero's Handbook**
**Top Tip 9:** Be prepared to change direction.

For the geographically challenged, this
can be an intense top tip. Is right
right? Or is left right? (Confusing,
I know.)

Marley had left a note for Poppy so she wouldn't
freak out if she returned to an empty house. I knew
the kind of effect that could have on a grown-up.

# P A N I C

*Note to you*
*Ellie was prone to panic and said it stood for:*
**Perfectly Acceptable Nuttiness In Crisis**
*but I don't think it does. Ellie makes things up all
the time. She says it keeps her mind agile.*

Not that Poppy was really a grown-up. She was
more like a grown-up in training. *We're all training to
be something,* I thought.

I'd sped-read Chapter 11 in *The Hero's Handbook*
before we set out and was thinking about how to be

conspicuously inconspicuous. Having Marley with us wasn't helping that. Three people were more conspicuous than two but we couldn't leave Marley behind. She was part of this mystery.

By the time we reached Bleachley Boulevard, the clouds had formed a thunderous mass in the sky. Rain was coming. That would definitely help us blend in.

No. 52, Fortescue's Antiquarian Book Collector, was tucked in between a supermarket and a department store. While the supermarket and department stores gleamed with fluorescent lights, like space stations in the night sky, Fortescue's was dark and dim, as though it had just arrived from the nineteenth century. Progress and change nudged and jostled Fortescue's from every angle, but it stood resolute. In fact, if you weren't looking for it, you might walk straight past it. It was the most inconspicuous shop I'd ever seen. It was the perfect destination for our clandestine mission.

I felt a chill of excitement. I was on a real Hero Hunt. Me. Hero Henrie. I smiled a little on the outside and *HOORAYED* loudly on the inside. Alex saw me smiling at myself and raised an eyebrow. His nonverbal communication was really improving.

## Note to you

*I'd made him read Chapter Five, "The Power of Nonverbal Communication," in **How to be Famous** by U.R.A. Mazeball. I couldn't wait to talk to him without saying a word.*

"Can't see a thing," said Marley, peering in the window. "I don't think they've ever cleaned these."

"Let's go in," said Alex.

He pushed the door and a bell tinkled as it opened. The air inside the shop was fusty and smelled like the nineteenth century. Dusty and old and forgotten.

The shop was stuffed with books, large shelves of them reaching up high, disappearing into the ceiling. It reminded me of the library at HoMe.

I had a sudden pang as HoMe made me think of Octavia Melchior. It was like a hunger pain but more painful because I knew eating couldn't help this kind of pain. Octavia was the closest I had come to my parents in nearly twelve years. He was my family, and I missed him, and all the things we would never say to each other.

"Hello?" said Marley. "Anyone here?"

We all jumped as a voice called out from under the large mahogany desk in front of us. "Hang on," said a man's voice. "Won't be a minute. Just picking my pea risotto off the floor."

A hand holding a pea popped up, and then a head, looking triumphant. It was attached to a young man with glasses, messy red hair and a big grin. He was wearing a suit that looked several sizes too big for him, as though he was dressing up in his dad's clothes. *Someone else in training?* I wondered.

"Pesky runaway pea," said the young man, squishing it between his two fingers. "It was hiding behind a pocket of dust. Give a pea an inch and it rolls a mile." He tilted his head to one side. "Hmm. I like that. Excuse me while I write it down."

He took a notebook out of his pocket and repeated the words as he wrote them down. "I like to collect the things I say that make me me. I put the best ones on Pinterest, with my pea illustrations." He chuckled. "I find myself endlessly fascinating sometimes. Don't you agree?"

Alex and I looked at each other. "We've only just met you so we don't really know how fascinating you are yet," I said.

"Well, you'll just have to take my word for it," he said.

"Are you Frederic Fortescue?" I said.

"No, that's my grandfather," said the young man, closing his notebook and putting it back in his suit.

"If it's okay, we'll wait for him," said Alex.

"You'll be waiting a long time, I'm afraid," said the young man. "He died five years ago."

"Oh, sorry," said Alex.

"That's okay," said the young man. "He was a great man, my Gramps." His grin disappeared when he said these words and his whole face changed.

"My grandfather died too," I said quietly.

The young man put his hand on my shoulder and I knew he understood even though he didn't say anything. Sometimes words can't say how you really feel.

"Gramps left me this shop," he said, wiping the dust off his knees, "and a few debts to boot. I could sell up and pay them all. And, believe me. I've considered it." He looked out the window. "You probably saw the supermarket and department store trying to squeeze me to death like a python."

"Yeah, we had to suck in our tummies before we entered your shop," I said.

He laughed. "Yes, it's skinny on the outside. But inside, well, Fortescue's been here for 200 years. You wouldn't believe the people who've been through these doors. The stories they've told. That kind of history can't be bought or sold. Some things are priceless."

*I guess HoMe is like that too*, I thought. *Part of my history. Part of me.*

"But where are my manners?" said the young man. "I'm Felix Fortescue. You can call me Felix."

Alex and I looked at each other. What else would we call him?

"I'm Henrie," I said, "and this is Alex."

"Hi, Felix. I'm Marley."

"Hello, Henrie, Alex and Marley-in-a-wheelchair," said Felix, checking out Marley's cast. "I broke my leg once." Felix and Marley smiled at each other. I frowned. Had everyone in the world broken a bone except me? It was like a Broken Bones Club.

"How did you break yours?" said Marley.

"I was Humpty Dumpty sitting on a wall," said Felix. "I was studying the mechanics of movement, of course, but my father was not amused by my Great Fall. He said I wasn't Humpty, I was Numpty.*"

He sort of smiled, but it was lopsided. Like it couldn't decide whether to be a smile or a grimace so it settled somewhere in between.

"But I'm sure you didn't come here to hear about my unresolved issues with my father. How can I help you? Are you looking for a book?"

"Maybe," said Marley.

"Or maybe not," I said. We didn't want to give too much away.

* "Numpty" is an old-fashioned word for an idiot.

90

*Note to you*
Not that we had too much to give away yet but **loose lips sink ships.** (I read that in a World War II spy story.)

Felix looked at Alex, then at me, then at Marley.

"Hmm, mysterious," he said, nodding.

"Very," said Marley.

"Well, I'm an excellent listener," said Felix. "You can trust me."

I decided on the spot that we could trust Felix. You just get a feeling about some people and I had a feeling about him. It might have been the freckles on his nose, or maybe his green eyes (same as me) and friendly smile.

## The Hero's Handbook
**Top Tip 33:** Don't try to reason with your intuition. It won't stand for it.

We filled Felix in as quickly as we could:

Heroes. HoMe. Agnes Hart. Fast Girl. Hieroglyphic message. Tiny key.

"Well, I don't know why that Fast Girl had my card," said Felix, when we'd finished, "but you've come to the right place for decoding messages. Gramps was a code breaker in World War II. A veritable whiz on everything from old-fashioned book ciphers to code-breaking machines like the Enigma. Though he always said the old coding ways were the best. He loved a bit of espionage till his dying day. He taught me lots of the tricks of his trade. We even made up our own language. It used to drive my father around the twist." Felix chuckled. I think he liked driving his father around the twist.

"Is it okay if we have a look around?" I said.

"Sure," said Felix. "I'll be in my office moving dwindling amounts of money between accounts if you need me."

"Thanks, Felix," I said.

"What are we looking for?" said Marley, when Felix had disappeared into his office.

"I don't know," I said. "But we'll know it when we see it."

Marley *harrumphed*.

"Have you got any better ideas?" I said.

"No," said Marley.

"I know it's like a needle in a haystack but Alex said a needle in a haystack is sharp," I said.

"Did you?" said Marley.

"Yeah," said Alex. "I did."

"You could put *that* on Pinterest," said Marley. "It's better than 'Give a pea an inch and it rolls a mile.'"

Alex grinned. I think he thought so too.

I wandered down a row of bookshelves:

### A–D

Books of all shapes and sizes were crammed together – subdued colors merging across spines. (Books from the Old Days seemed to be gray or green or brown.)

When I got to the **D** books, I spied a title that looked familiar.

I picked it off the shelf. I was sure I'd seen a really old edition like this in the library at HoMe. I knew it was a very famous book by a very famous author so maybe it was just a coincidence. Maybe every bookshop in the world had this book? Maybe it was like the Bible? Or the dictionary?

But what if it wasn't?

Maybe Penelope Fuggleton was right: there are no such things as coincidences.

I was still holding the book, thinking, when Felix spoke suddenly behind me.

"Gramps operated this as a quasi library as well," he said, seeing the book in my hand. "It's a great story, that one. I'm a big Dickens fan. *Bleak House* is my favorite though. So full of fog. If you ever want to borrow a book, write your name on the card at the back. Old school, I know, but I'm like Gramps. I like the old ways, even though most people don't. And I feel like, somehow, they keep him alive in the shop."

I smiled at Felix. I liked the way he thought. I felt like that sometimes too. Out of step with things and people around me. Ellie said we all had to find our own step but it was lonely walking by myself sometimes.

Felix opened the back of the book to show me the lending card I should fill in if I ever took a book.

About halfway up the card, I spied a familiar name:

## Octavia Melchior 22 July 1946.

My thoughts began to power up. Agnes contacted Octavia for help in 1946, and Octavia's name was in a book in Frederic's shop in 1946. Together, they formed a straight line of connection.

## Agnes ⟶ Octavia ⟶ Frederic

My brain was fizzing with possibilities as I repeated their names over and over in my head.

But **how?** And most importantly **why?**

We hadn't found any answers yet.

Just a whole lot more questions.

It was time to say goodbye to Felix but I was sure we'd be seeing him again. Because of his grandfather, he'd just become important to the mystery somehow. And I liked him. I knew we could trust someone whose name meant "happy" or "lucky."

As we left, I turned to him.

"Can I put a poster in your window, please?" I said, opening my bag. I'd been working on some posters all night.

"Of course," he said. "It will cover up some of the dirt."

Felix read the poster. "Why caramel shortbread?" he said.

"My mum loves it," I said.

"Me too," said Felix.

We said goodbye to Felix and walked along Bleachley Boulevard back to Marley's house, thinking deep thoughts.

### Note to you
Well, my thoughts were deep. I don't know about Marley and Alex. They were probably thinking about food.

As we paused at a set of traffic lights, I thought I glimpsed the *swish* of a black coat around a corner, like the flap of a bat's wing, but when I looked again, the corner was just a corner.

We had a few hours left before we had to meet Ellie and Alex's dad back at Marley's place. Ellie had texted me to say they were still at the Super Sleuth Association, filling in forms about the mission.

I was thinking about Octavia's name in the Charles Dickens book in Frederic's shop. Agnes, Octavia and Frederic. How did they all fit together? I thought about Alex, Marley and me. We were all different but linked too by HoMe and a mystery. Maybe that was the same for Agnes, Octavia and Frederic?

I told Marley and Alex about Octavia's name in the book.

"So Octavia knew Frederic?" said Marley.

"He must have," I said. "Let's look at what we know so far."

"That won't take long," said Marley.

"Mysteries aren't solved in minutes," I said.

"I guess," said Marley. "It's just that Penelope Fuggleton solves hers in sizzling, heart-stopping seconds."

I seethed on the inside. Penelope Fuggleton had a lot to answer for.

"So we know that Agnes wanted to contact HoMe about something," I said. "So what if she did and she actually met up with Octavia?"

"And he was helping her," said Marley. "So *he* might have written down information about her mystery somewhere."

"How can we find out if he did?" said Alex.

"Octavia would have written it in the Hero Book," I said. "Every mission was written up there. But I've seen the present Hero Book at HoMe and it only goes back a year. We'd have to look at the book with records for 1946."

"That's more than seventy years ago," said Alex. "Where would that be now?"

"I don't know," I said.

"Who would know?" said Marley.

Alex and I both answered at the same time: "Albert Abernathy."

## Chapter Seven
# An Old Foe

I **ARRIVED AT** the café on Lawson Street half an hour later, after arranging to meet Albert Abernathy. He had answered my call immediately. Almost as if he'd been sitting on the phone, waiting for it.

Alex and Marley were sitting at a table in the window of a café across the road so they could see me.

"Eyes on, GREENPEA," said Alex through the walkie-talkie.

"Roger that, MIMI," I replied. Then I stuffed the walkie-talkie in my backpack and pushed open the door of the café.

Café Lawson was busy with people queuing for their coffees and reading newspapers. The café was toasty and the smell of freshly baked cookies tickled my nostrils. *Yum.* Chocolate chip. My favorite.

I breathed in the aroma, and scanned the room.

I had wanted to get there first so I could watch Albert Abernathy arrive.

Tucked into the far corner was a familiar figure in an impeccable suit and tie. Albert Abernathy. Of course, he was there before me. He was always a step, or two, or three ahead. He didn't have to gain the upper hand. He *was* the upper hand.

I had had a feeling he was going to pop back into my life again, somehow, somewhere, but I didn't think *I'd* be the one trying to find him. Life can be like that. Leading you in all kinds of swirly, twirly directions. It can make you very dizzy. I was spinning now as everything that had happened at HoMe only three days ago came rushing back at me.

"Ah, Henrie," said Albert Abernathy, looking up from his tea and crossword. "Very punctual. So rare in the young these days. How delightful to see you."

"You didn't seem very surprised to hear from me," I said, sitting down opposite him.

"I like to expect the unexpected," he said as he

stirred his tea. "In that way, the unexpected never really is."

"Never really is what?" I said.

"Unexpected," he said.

I'd forgotten how curly his words could be. Never quite traveling in a straight line. He liked his words to play **peekab00**. With you. And me.

"Besides," he said, "I knew we'd meet again."

"You did?" I said.

"You found the Control Center?" he said.

## Note to you
The old answering a question with a question.

I nodded and thought of the acrostic note within a note he'd left, telling us where the Control Center was. In the heart of HoMe. Behind Phineas Melchior's portrait. I should probably thank him but that didn't feel quite right. I'd found what he'd wanted me to find. Once again, he was controlling things. But why?

Ellie said he was an opportunist. Was this just another opportunity for him?

"I did," I said. "I guess I should say '*thank you*.'"

"But it doesn't feel quite right to say that, does it, Henrie?" He smiled.

I checked out his teeth. He still seemed to have

more than usual but the sharp ones didn't look quite so sharp today.

"Your grandfather would be very proud of you," he said. "You are surprisingly like him, you know." He took another sip of his tea. "If only Octavia had had the chance to discover this for himself. But, sadly, time does not wait for things to unfold as we would like them to."

He lowered his head as he said this and his words sounded different. Kind of low to the ground. Not pumped up by trickiness or planning or thinking of what came next. They sounded as if, maybe, he really meant them.

He looked up at me. His eyes were penetrating and his gaze was wily. Or, maybe not. The old Albert Abernathy was back.

"What can I do for you, Henrie?" he said.

"I need information about someone," I said.

"I see you are discovering that information is valuable," he said. "And who is this person you seek?"

"An archaeologist called Agnes Hart," I said.

There was a flicker in his eyes. Just for a second. A flash of recognition.

*He's heard the name before*, I thought.

Of course, he would never tell me this directly.

"And what of Miss Hart?" he said.

"I need to know if she rang HoMe many years

ago. And if she did, why she did and if there was any follow-up about her case."

"You want to see the Hero Book records from 1946," he said.

# ALERT ALERT ALERT ALERT ALERT ALERT ALERT ALERT ALERT ALERT

Okay, I'm going to stop right there. Did you hear what I heard?

Albert Abernathy just made **a great big mistake.** I couldn't believe my ears. Albert Abernathy didn't make mistakes.

Do you know what it was?

◯ YES

Excellent sleuthing. Congratulations.
You could become a hero in training.

◯ NO

Not so excellent sleuthing. Commiserations. Do you
have any excuse at all for your poor observation
skills? Do you have wax in your ears? Sleep in your
eyes? Are you having a brain freeze? **WAKE UP.**

You see, I hadn't mentioned how long ago it was. Albert Abernathy *did* know something.

"Yes, do you have them?" I said, cooler than a cucumber ...

### Note to you

Or as zen as a zucchini; as poised as a pumpkin; as languid as a leek. Choose the vegetable you like best.

... even though on the inside I was shouting, **AHA! GOT YOU.**

"No, but I can access them for you," he said.

"And will you?" I said.

"I will," he said. "But–"

I knew there'd be a "But." Nothing was straightforward with Albert Abernathy.

"But what?" I said.

"There may be a time when I need you to help me," he said, leaning into me.

I leaned back. Albert Abernathy was a personal-space invader.

"When that time comes," he said, "can I count on you?"

"I ... guess," I said, my words slow and heavy.

He smiled at me. "Oh, Henrie. I'm afraid that response will not suffice. '*I guess*' is a neither-here-nor-there answer. I need a *'Yes.'* Or a *'No.'* An absolute is the only known."

*But it's not,* I thought. *I don't know.* He was asking me to agree to something without knowing what I was agreeing to. How could he ask for an absolute when I had no idea of the shape of the thing? That wasn't fair, was it? It might be something really **terrible.** Or **horrible**. Or **disastrous.** Or **dangerous.** How could I agree to something that could be **catastrophic?**

"I promise you it won't cause any harm," he said, reading my hesitation.

"Do you know what it is?" I said.

He smiled. "Yes. And no."

The old *Yes* and *No* again. His favorite way of answering a question. Was he evil or good? Was he both?

But we really needed that information about Agnes Hart. I didn't have a choice.

"Okay," I said. "I agree to help you."

"Excellent," he said. "I believe you will keep your word. You have the integrity of a Melchior. I'll email you the information you require by the end of the day." He paused and looked right into my eyes. "Is there anything else you wish to ask me, Henrie?" he said.

"You know there is," I said. It was the biggest question of them all. I knew he knew what it was but he didn't speak. He was going to make me ask him.

"Do you know where my parents are?" I said.

"Do you think I would have kept that vital information from you?" he said.

He was answering a question with a question again.

If he could do it so could I.

"Isn't that what you do?" I said.

He chuckled. "Oh, very good, Henrie. You are learning quickly. I have so enjoyed our talk." He paused. "You are right to be suspicious," he said. "Never trust too easily. People are seldom as they seem." He stood up, straightening his jacket. "Goodbye, Henrie. Until we meet again."

I sat there for a few minutes after he'd gone. Then I noticed he'd left his newspaper. I grabbed it and stood up to run after him but my eye caught a familiar word and I stopped. I zoned in on one of the crossword clues and his answer:

12 across: *One of the three wise kings who was said to have visited the baby Jesus (8).*

I looked at Albert Abernathy's answer: Melchior.

I thought of the diary entry we'd found in the hankie holder and Agnes's words: *"His name means King."*

Agnes Hart *had* met Octavia Melchior.

# I knew it.

And Albert Abernathy knew it too.

Even when he was helping me, there was something undefined about Albert Abernathy. I still couldn't see the shape of him, and that didn't make me feel good.

I had a bad feeling in my heart.

True to his word, Albert Abernathy emailed me later that afternoon:

Dear Henrie,

I am attaching a copy of the record pertaining to Agnes Hart and her inquiry to HoMe. I hope it provides you with the information you seek.

Albert Abernathy

I opened the attachment:

# Agnes Hart, 12 July 1946

**Description:** In 1922, the Egyptological Society of Archaeologists (ESA) accused Miss Hart of stealing a priceless gold statue of Akhenaten, Tutankhamen's father – unearthed in the outer chamber of Tutankhamen's tomb. She was never officially charged and her guilt or innocence was never fully determined. She has subsequently remained under a long shadow of suspicion. She has alluded to extenuating circumstances but due to the delicate nature of these will elaborate upon them only in person. The statue is still missing.

**Assignment grade:** Gold.

**Action:** Meeting arranged between Octavia Melchior and Agnes Hart.

**Outcome:** Agnes Hart revealed vital, extraordinary information but due to the Official Secrets Act both parties agreed that we must now proceed with caution. We will communicate via a third party to ensure safety and security.

## Chapter Eight

# Bad News and More Bad News

**OH NO. AGNES** was accused of stealing a priceless statue.

I don't know what I was expecting but not this.

And now I had to break the bad news to Marley.

*Note to you*

*There is no good way to break bad news.*
*It shatters every which way and pieces fly far.*
*Weeks later, you will still find splinters of them in unexpected places.*

Marley was in the kitchen with Alex, getting afternoon tea ready. She looked up as I walked into the room.

"Have you got the email?" she said.

I nodded. And screwed up my face.

### Note to you

U.R.A. Mazeball said a screwed-up face is shorthand for: It's bad. Worse than you could imagine.

"It's bad, isn't it?" said Marley. "Worse than I could imagine?"

I nodded. So far so good. Now for the really bad bit. I took a big breath and my words rushed out. "Agnes was accused of stealing something from the tomb of Tutankhamen," I said. "A gold statue of Tut's father, Akhenaten."

Marley was pale. "No, that can't be right. I don't believe it. Agnes would never do that."

"I'm so sorry, Marley," I said. "I know it's hard to believe that someone in your family is a thief but maybe Agnes was the black sheep of the family? I've got a whole herd of black sheep in my family."

"Don't call her a thief," said Marley.

"You didn't really know her," I said.

"Neither did you," said Marley. "But I know what Mum told me about her and Agnes was good and kind and true. She loved being an archaeologist and she would never **ever** steal from a dig. That's totally

111

against the archaeologist's code of ethics."

I nodded. Heroes had ethics too.

"Well, someone stole it," said Alex.

"And hid it," I said. "And kept it hidden for all these years. Until everyone thought it was lost and forgot about it."

"Everyone except Agnes," said Marley. "Right until her dying day. *'The truth never perishes.'* That's what she meant. She was innocent. And we're going to prove it."

If Poppy was surprised to see Marley having afternoon tea with four guests, she wasn't surprised enough to take off her headphones. They were probably fused to her ears.

She nodded at me as she unpacked the grocery bags, humming away to the beat of her head.

Over tea and cupcakes, we filled Ellie and Timothy Fischer in on everything that had happened.

"Curious," said Timothy Fischer, when we'd finished. "I've been to the Museum of Antiquities. It has inventories of all the items discovered on archaeological digs. Maybe that will reveal something?"

"Why does Octavia mention the Official Secrets Act, Dad?" said Alex.

"Yes, that's curious too," said Timothy Fischer, frowning. "Your aunt wasn't involved in any kind of espionage during World War I, was she, Marley?"

"Espionage!" said Marley. "You mean she might be a thief *and* a spy?"

"We're just thinking out loud, Marley," said Ellie. "But the Official Secrets Act often related to national security and espionage during times of war."

*Espionage.* The word breathed through me like a secret.

Felix had said his grandfather was a code cracker during World War II – a different war but a war nonetheless. Was that important? I wrote the word down in my notebook and it shimmered on the page – full of mystery and possibility.

## espionage

"I'll see if I can find out if there's any chatter on the underground airwaves at the Super Sleuth Association," said Timothy Fischer. "Something's prompted all this recent interest in Agnes Hart."

I looked at Ellie hopefully but she shook her head. "I'm sorry, Henrie," she said. "The lawyer wasn't much help. The last address for Max and Persey was in Prague nine years ago but they could be anywhere by now. They haven't been in contact with her since. They seem to have … vanished."

*Vanished.*

"I'm putting posters up around town asking if anyone has seen them," I said. "Someone might tell someone who tells someone who tells someone who tells someone who tells someone … and the question hops across the world and finally reaches someone who knows them."

"Like a game of telephone," said Marley.

"Sort of," I said. "But hopefully more reliable."

We played telephone at school once and "I come from Sweden" ended up as "My eye is bleeding." It only takes one word to bend and break and alarm the whole sentence with a different meaning. You could be asking about life in Sweden, or calling for an ambulance.

Mrs. Petrie said whispers were wobbly structures. Not like DNA or bones. They were far more sturdy.

"We're going to do everything we can," said Ellie.

"We all are," said Timothy Fischer. "I've got my mates at the SSA helping too. The more noise we can make, the more chance Max and Persey might hear us."

I liked everyone including my mum and dad

in the conversation. It made everything feel normal, and as if they were part of our group too. Not strangers who were my closest blood relatives but who'd disappeared the day I was born.

Sometimes I looked at myself in the mirror and held up a baby photo, trying to see the baby in me. I'd changed a lot since I was born.

What if Mum and Dad didn't recognize me? What if they walked right past me on the street one day and we never ever knew who we were to each other? I shook that thought away. First of all, we had to help Marley.

"Let's split up," I said. "Alex, Marley and I will go to the Museum of Antiquities to see if we can find out more information about Agnes and the stolen statue."

"And we'll see what we can find out about Agnes and any wartime activities," said Ellie. "Oh, and one more thing. HoMe's lawyer said she's had a request to use HoMe's training rooms for an International Relations conference that needs a late change of venue. Is that okay with everyone? It might as well be used for something until you decide what to do with it."

"Fine with me," I said.

"Us too," said Timothy Fischer.

We synchronized our watches, and said we'd meet back at Marley's in three hours.

The Inventory Section in the Museum of Antiquities was the only door without a queue. I guess rows and rows of tall gray filing cabinets weren't as fascinating as glimpses of times past.

"Can I help you?" said a woman at the main desk, looking surprised to see us. I don't think she'd said those words in a while.

"Yes, please," I said. "We're looking for the inventory list from a dig in 1922 – from Tutankhamen's tomb."

"Of course you are," she said. "It's the only dig anyone's ever interested in. The entire Egyptian civilization overshadowed by Tutankhamen – a kid who wasn't even a pharaoh for that long." She sighed. "But you're in luck. We finished digitizing those records last year." She scrolled through a file on her computer. "Now, let me see, yes, here it is. Do you want a printout?"

"That'd be great, please," I said. "Thanks so much for your help."

### Note to you
Ellie said you can never be too polite. Politeness spreads happiness.

The woman smiled at me as she waited at the printer. "But it *is* good to see kids doing some real research. Not just relying on Wikipedia for information. Is this for a school project?"

"Yes," I said. "We're thinking of becoming virtual archaeologists."

"Well, good for you," she said as she handed me the printout. "I think."

We huddled around the printout, reading through all the treasures. There were more than 3000 things listed in Tut's tomb for his journey to the afterlife. He'd have to pay excess baggage if he was traveling with all that stuff in *this* life. It took us a while to go through it all.

At the end, we all looked at each other.

"Weird," I said. "The statue's not listed there."

"It must be," said Marley. "Look again."

We read it again. Lists of jewelry, statues, chairs, couches, musical instruments, vases, clothes, perfume, thrones, chariots, lamps and so much more blurring into each other.

"Nope," said Alex. "Still not there. Maybe Agnes was in charge of writing everything up and she left it off deliberately because she'd already stolen it."

"That's horrible," said Marley. "How can you say that?"

"I'm just thinking of the worst-case scenario," said Alex. "Someone has to."

"Why does someone have to?" said Marley.

"Because even though we want to, we can't ignore the evidence that is pointing Agnes's way."

"Well, think of a worst worst-case scenario that doesn't make Agnes a thief," said Marley.

Marley and I looked at Alex.

"Well?" said Marley.

"Still thinking," said Alex.

Marley glared at Alex and he glared back.

"Come on, you two," I said, breaking their glare-off. "We're not getting anywhere here. Let's check out the Egyptian section. We might learn something about Akhenaten's statue there."

We wandered through the Egyptian section of the museum. It was quieter now. A gaggle of schoolkids had just left with a frazzled teacher, counting off the kids as they bolted past her through the door and shouting at them to, "Slow down. Buddy up. Bus outside. **Oskar, put that mummy down!**"

I spied a hieroglyphic scroll in a glass case, and read the caption to the right of it:

Akhenaten was one of the most powerful pharaohs in Egypt. He ruled for seventeen years.

Someone had left some notes marked **CONFIDENTIAL** on a stand next to the case. I had a quick look behind me and then picked up the notes. I was a hero on a hunt and heroes had to snoop sometimes.

It was all pretty boring at first: new hand towels for the kitchen on Level 3. A complaint from someone in archives about the standard of cookie in the tearoom.

But then I did see something interesting. A copy of an email from the museum director about a new exhibition.

---

### Re: NEW EXHIBITION OF AKHENATEN

There is a renewed worldwide effort to find the missing gold statue of Akhenaten for this exhibition. The statue was reportedly stolen from Tutankhamen's tomb by archaeologist Agnes Hart. Miss Hart died in 1980 proclaiming her innocence. Adding further doubt to her innocence is the rumor that she was a German spy in the period between the First and Second World Wars although, once again, this claim was never substantiated. If we are approached by media for comment, the response should be, without exception: NO COMMENT. Please ensure that all museum personnel are aware that they should not repeat any unsubstantiated accusations.

---

**Oh no!** This was catastrophic. Agnes – a German spy. Marley would be devastated. **Again.**

But a new exhibition. This was important information. It would explain why there was all this interest in the statue now. And Agnes.

I had to tell Alex and Marley.

I thought they were looking at different exhibits in other corners of the room but I couldn't see them anywhere. I was alone in the Mummy Room. Well, apart from all the mummies, of course. And the coffins and funerary masks. And the mummified cats and dogs, and one very long crocodile.

But I was definitely the only living and breathing thing in sight.

"Marley? Alex?" I said. "Where are you? Stop messing around. This isn't funny." My words echoed around me. I checked my watch. The museum would be closing soon. We had to get back to meet Ellie and Timothy Fischer.

I turned on my walkie-talkie. "Are you receiving, TIBS?" I said. Static crackled back at me. Radio silence all around.

I looked up as I heard footsteps at the other end of the room. *There they are.*

I ran toward the sound but there was no one there. As I turned in confusion, someone was suddenly standing behind me. Standing really close and pressing something into my ribs. A ruler?

A knife? A size 9 knitting needle? Whatever it was, it was very sharp and pointy.

**I gasped.**

# Chapter Nine

# Things Turn Villainous

**"STAY STILL,"** said a voice, a girl's. "If you want to see your friends again, do as I tell you. Do you understand? Nod once for yes and twice for no."

I nodded once for yes.

"Good," she said. "At least you can count. The last kid I kidnapped was hopeless at math."

*The last kid she kidnapped!*

"I–" I said.

"No," she said, jabbing me in the ribs with the ruler, knife or size 9 knitting needle. "*I* speak. *You* listen. Got it? Nod once for yes and twice for no."

I nodded once for yes.

"Do you think that works, though?" she said. "Once for yes and twice for no? Or should it be the other way round? Once for no and twice for yes. **Yes** is more emphatic so maybe it should be two nods for **Yes. Yes.** What do you think?"

"I–" I said.

"I told you not to speak," she said, her voice low and slow. "That was a trick to catch you out and you fell right into it." She pushed me. "Walk. Don't turn around. Keep going until I tell you to stop."

I nodded twice. *Oops.* I shook my head. That wasn't right. I meant to nod once. Not twice.

The girl sighed. "I knew it was too good to be true."

We walked slowly down the hall. My heart was pounding and questions were crashing in my head: *Who was this girl? Where were Marley and Alex? What was happening?*

As we turned the corner at the end, I saw a guard, slumped in a chair by the door to the Rosetta Stone exhibition. I thought he was asleep but he pulled himself up when he saw us approaching. I had to get his attention somehow. Signal to him that I was in trouble. That I needed HELP.

**The Hero's Handbook**
**Top Tip 48:** In a tricky situation, be inventive. Use whatever you can get your hands on.

I didn't have much. But ... hands! I had two of those. Plus ten fingers.

I started tapping SOS with my middle finger. Over and over on my sleeve, the rhythm of the *short long shorts* flowing through me like a jitter.

"Nice try," the girl whispered in my ear, placing her free hand over my finger and gripping it tight.

*Ouch!*

"You can stop now. Your SOS signals are wasted on that loaf of a guard."

I looked at the guard. He *did* look a little doughy and unrisen. He was also covered in bread crumbs from the half-eaten sandwich sticking out of his front pocket.

We were level with him now. This was my last chance. I had to do ... something. Make an impression. So he'd remember us. When people came looking for me.

I pretended to stumble and tried to bend over my shoes – as if I needed to tie my shoelaces – but the girl pulled me back up to my feet. I struggled as much as I could in her pincer grasp.

"Everything all right there?" said the guard, sitting up higher in his chair.

"Oh yes, good afternoon, officer," said the girl in a light bouncy voice. "Just taking my little sister to see the mummies." She sighed. Dramatically. "You know what kids are like. Just wanting to be on their screens. Practically have to drag them kicking and screaming toward knowledge."

The guard grinned. "I do," he said. "You've no idea the things I see here. Kids ignoring all the wonder around them. Lost in their own heads. Texting on their phones." He looked at me with a serious expression. "History teaches you about the world, young lady. I hope you learn something today."

"Yes, sir, thank you, sir," I said, "and if you see a tall boy and a girl in a—"

"Oh, sis," said the girl, cutting me off. "This nice man is much too busy and important to convey messages to your friends."

The guard blushed. "Well, it's true I am rather busy with this new exhibition." He straightened his tie and hat. "I shouldn't really be saying this but you're only kids so …" He looked around but the corridor was empty, "… we're expecting a rather important delivery in a couple of days. I've never seen the bosses so excited and *hush-hush*. Closed doors. Whispered asides. Significant looks. I'm very observant, you know. There's not a lot that gets by me. They don't call me Lookout Len for nothing, you know."

"I bet they don't," said the girl. "A new delivery? That's exciting. Where's it coming from?"

"I'm afraid that information is classified," said Lookout Len, puffing out his chest and trying to stuff the sandwich back in his pocket.

"Of course," said the girl. "I understand. Classified information must be sealed tight. My mum and dad run their own company and they said only the rarest kind of noble employee can be trusted with *that* kind of information."

"That's exactly right," said Lookout Len. "Of course, I *am* that rare and noble kind of employee. My mind is like a sausage machine."

"I can see that," said the girl. "You can tell how important some people are just by looking at them."

Lookout Len seemed to be getting taller as the girl spoke. He was nearly as tall as Alex now.

"Well, great to chat, Lookout Len, if it's okay to call you that?" said the girl, giving me a little push.

"Of course, Miss," said Lookout Len. "You may. And, indeed, you have."

"Good luck with that Top Secret Delivery," said the girl.

"Thank you, Miss," said Lookout Len. "You and the public at large can rest assured that the museum is in good hands."

"That's such a relief to know," said the girl. "Goodbye, Lookout Len."

"Goodbye," he said. "Don't forget: tell everyone the museum is being guarded by the strongest and the best."

"*As if*," said the girl, when we were out of his hearing. "The museum's in trouble if *he's* the best. But *you* were more useful than I thought. Maybe I should use kids as props more often?"

"Where are my friends?" I said.

"Safe," she said. "For the moment. But make just one mistake and you'll never see them again. Got it?"

"Yes," I said. I thought it was safer to speak than nod. I didn't want to get my **Yes** and **No** wrong again. For Alex and Marley's sake.

We walked through the museum for another five minutes until we came to a long, dark corridor – loud with silence.

"Stop here," said the girl. We were standing in front of a small room. She unlocked the door, pushed me in and turned on a light by the door.

The room was stacked high with boxes of exhibits, yet to be unpacked. They had come from all over the world. I could see labels from Brazil, Africa and Egypt. And as I gazed around the room I saw Marley and Alex at the end of it. Alex was sitting on one of the boxes and Marley was next to him – resting her broken leg on another.

I ran to them. They both looked very pleased to see me.

"Are you okay?" I said.

"We're fine," said Alex. "But no thanks to her."

"Yeah, she tricked us into coming in here," said Marley, pointing at the girl.

"It was so easy," said the girl, yawning.

"And then she locked us in," said Alex.

"We banged on the door for ages," said Marley.

"Well, I told you not to bother," said the girl. "This part of the museum is closed to the public. No one can hear you scream down here."

We all stared at the girl. She was younger than I'd first thought. Maybe around Poppy's age. Sixteen? She was dressed in a long black leather coat, with matching gloves. She had shoulder-length black hair, dark eyebrows raised at an inquiring angle, and piercing blue eyes. Which were staring at me.

"Okay," she said. "Spill the beans. Who are you?"

"Who are *you*?" I said.

"Oh, I love this game," she said, sitting on top of a box and crossing her legs. "Shall we make it ten questions? Okay, I'll start: Where is it?"

"Where's what?" said Marley.

"Akhenaten's gold statue," she said. "Lost to history for nearly 100 years but now the hottest piece of Egyptology on the market."

"Because of the new exhibition," I said.

"Correct," said the girl. "Everyone's looking for it but it's got my name on it."

"What *is* your name?" I said.

"You're right," she said. "As we are all in this tangle of a treasure hunt, let's introduce ourselves. I'll go first. I'm Violetta Villarne, that's pronounced 'arn' as in 'yarn,' if you like knitting, or 'barn,' if you prefer cows, which you bumpkins probably do." She paused and looked at us hopefully. "You may have heard of me?"

We all shook our heads and mumbled, "Sorry. No. Never. Not even a whisper."

She sighed. "Oh, well. That's because I'm so successfully secretive in my work."

"What is your work?" said Alex.

"I'm a VO," said Violetta Villarne.

"A VO?" I said.

"A VillInc Operative," said the girl.

"VillInc?" I said.

"Villains Incorporated," she said.

"Villains Incorporated?" I said.

"Are you going to repeat everything I say?" she said.

"Only the shocking stuff," I said.

"So you've heard of VillInc?" said Violetta Villarne,
looking hopeful again.

We all shook our heads and mumbled again, "Sorry. No. Never. Not even a whisper."

She sighed again. "Oh well. Your turn."

"I'm Alex Fischer," said Alex.

"Marley Hart," said Marley.

"Henrie Melchior," I said.

"I know who you all are already, of course," said the girl. "And you two interest me greatly." She looked at Marley then me, and turned to Alex, dismissing him with her hand. "You, not so much. And YOU," she swung back to Marley. "You owe me money. Lots of it. Do you have any idea how much it costs to repair Italian leather?"

"Well, you shouldn't have been trying to break into my house," said Marley.

"How else was I going to get it?" said the girl.

"Get what?" I said.

"Okay, cards on the table," said the girl, sidestepping that question. "What do you know?"

"What do *you* know?" I said.

The girl laughed. "I know *you* don't know very much. You're bumbling through this mystery like Tweedledees and Tweedledums."

"Is your name really Violetta Villarne?" said Marley.

"Do you have a problem with that, Hart rhymes with Fart?" said Violetta Villarne.

"It's just it sounds so ... villainous," said Marley.

"And your point?" said Violetta Villarne. "Because in my line of business, that *is* the point."

"What is your line of business?" I said.

"Isn't that obvious?" said Violetta Villarne. "Villainy."

"You mean you're a thief," said Alex.

"Oh, I am liking you even less, Fischer rhymes with ... Swisher," said Violetta Villarne.

### Note to you

It's hard to find a word that rhymes with Fischer. But even harder to find one that rhymes with Melchior. Let me know if you think of one.

"That statue is not yours to sell," said Marley.

"It wasn't your aunt's to steal either," said Violetta Villarne. "Oh, yes, I know all about Thieving Agnes Hart. She's quite a hero among villains." She laughed.

"Agnes didn't steal it," said Marley, going red in the face and stamping her non-plastered foot. "How many times do I have to say that?"

"Whatever," said Violetta Villarne. "It doesn't interest me who stole it. It interests me who has it. And from where I'm standing, you three are looking like the ones who have the answer to that."

"Well, we don't," said Alex. "We're looking for it too."

"Then why don't I believe you?" she said. "VillInc has a client who will pay substantially for this artifact and we don't intend to lose this sale." She suddenly smiled at us and stood up. "But you know what? This is good. I like you. Well, two of you, anyway." She glared at Alex and he glared back. "You're a step up from the usual pea brains I encounter. I could do with some apprentices. What do you say? How about becoming villains? You could take the Villain Test. But I warn you: standards are exceptional. I scored 200 percent on my first Villain Test."

"How can you score 200 percent?" said Marley.

"I gave additional answers for every question," said Violetta. "The examiners said they'd never seen such willingness to be villainous. But it's hardly surprising. I am a third-generation villain. My Great-Uncle Merton was as evil as they come. He always left a calling card at the scene: an $\mathbf{M}$, sliced in half and spotted with blood.

"Even villains were nervous of GUM, especially after he lost his two front teeth trying to bite a sword in half. He was unstoppable. The teeth are still in the sword. It hangs up in the assembly hall at Villains' School to encourage us all to achieve the impossible."

# The Villain Test

1) Do you plot bad deeds at breakfast?
2) Are you constantly devising new ways
   to be sneaky? In fact, you could fill a book
   on sneakiness?
3) Is your favorite word DEVIOUS?
4) Do you aspire toward chaos?
5) Do you pickpocket everything you see?
   Even this test?

## Answers

### Five out of five
CONGRATULATIONS:
You are vilely villainous. Remove this test from
your pocket and put it back on the desk. Excellent
pickpocketing. You are a natural.

### One to Four
COMMISERATIONS:
You are not a villain. You will never be a villain. Stop
reading the Villain Test now. We can hear the sound
of your heart spluttering with fear. It's deafening.

"Villains' School?" I said.

"Of course," she said. "Even villains need to learn. Ignorance is unacceptable. So, are you tempted by the test?" she said.

"No, thanks," I said. "We're heroes in training."

"But the Hero World is *so* boring," she said, yawning. "It's no fun at all. Don't you want to be like me? Dramatic. Stylish. And rich – with oodles of money in offshore bank accounts? Money, money, money. Falling from trees like autumn leaves. I could make your dreams come true."

She looked at Marley. "Imagine a wheelchair with turbocharged wheels and power steering."

I could see Marley disappearing momentarily in an imagined haze of turbocharged wheels and power steering.

She looked at Alex. "Imagine a skateboard with hovercraft wings and aerodynamic lift."

I could see Alex disappearing momentarily in an imagined haze of hovercraft wings and aerodynamic lift.

She looked at me. "But, you, Henrie Melchior. You, I think, will be harder to impress. Am I right?"

She walked over to one of the exhibits and studied the shipping label. "Money gives you power to ship archaeological finds from all around the world. To fill museums with treasures. To feel you have conquered just a small piece of history for yourself. But one of the best things money can buy is ... information. Important information denied to you by other sources. And I think maybe information is what you seek most, Henrie. Am I right? Possibly information about ... let me guess ... your parents?"

Her piercing blue eyes seemed to be pulling something deep inside me, yanking it out with force and leaving me breathless.

"My parents?" I said. "Do you know something about them? What? How? Why?"

A small smile flitted across her face. The satisfied smile of someone who had just gotten what she wanted.

"So many questions," she said. "Everything will be revealed in time. But first, we need to strike a bargain. You and me. I presume you're in charge of this motley lot?"

"Well, we haven't exactly elected a leader yet," said Alex, "and I–"

"What kind of bargain?" I said, interrupting him.

"An exchange of talents," said Violetta. "Yours and mine. What do you say, Henrie Melchior?"

I didn't need to think.

"Yes," I said, nodding lots and lots of times.

"I say yes."

## Note to you

Don't panic. Keep reading.

# Chapter Ten
# Watch Out. Villain About.

**ALEX AND MARLEY** were looking at me with their mouths wide open.

"Henrie!" said Marley. "What are you doing?"

I did my best nonverbal communication for DON'T WORRY. I'VE GOT A PLAN – raising one eyebrow, lowering the other and making my eyes meet in the middle – but Marley and Alex just looked puzzled by my face.

"Let's get going," said Violetta Villarne. "We've got a statue to find."

Alex and Marley began to head toward the door, but Violetta turned and said to them, "Not you two."

"What?" said Alex.

"You heard," said Violetta. "You're staying here."

Before Alex could say anything else she pushed me out the door into the corridor. Then she locked the door behind her.

Alex and Marley began to bang on it furiously. We could hear their muffled cries of *LET US OUT. LET US OUT.*

Violetta Villarne laughed. "They won't keep that up for long."

"But you can't leave them in there," I said.

"I can and I am," said Violetta Villarne. "I have no further use for them. They'd slow us down. Besides, I don't like working in groups. Villains are NOT team players. We're lone wolves. Out for ourselves in the hunt."

She grinned as she said this and looked as hungry as a wolf. We were both on a hunt. A villain and a hero. But she had all the power at the moment. I had to think fast.

"Well," I said, "you've forgotten something."

"I have?" she said, frowning. "That's very unlike me. What?"

"We're kids so people know where we are and they're expecting us home. If we don't turn up when we're supposed to, they'll miss us and raise the alarm. And then they'll come looking for us." I paused. "And you too."

She sighed. "All right. All right. You are such a nag. I'll leave the key in the door to give your friends a chance. They'll work it out eventually with the old-push-it-out-so-it-falls-onto-paper-pushed-under-the-door trick. Or not. It's up to them."

"They will. They're smart."

"But before I do that," said Violetta Villarne. "Give me the key."

"What key?" I said.

"The teeny-weeny one you found in Agnes's embroidery box," she said.

What? How did she know about that? We'd only told a few people about the key. Unless Marley's house was bugged. Could that be?

"Well," said Violetta Villarne, "I'm waiting. It's a simple transaction. The key for your friends in exchange for Agnes's key."

I didn't have a choice.

Slowly, I handed over Agnes's key and watched as she put the key in the lock to the exhibits room. I hoped Marley and Alex would think of looking through the keyhole to see if it was there.

"By the way," said Violetta Villarne, "we should exchange business cards." She handed me hers. "It might surprise you how often people – even heroes – need villains. We're in great demand."

I shuddered at her words, and looked at the card in my hand. At first, all I could see was red because every single letter on it was written in bright-red type.

I knew what that meant. **Red spelled danger.** Like FIRE raging out of control, or a flow of red-hot burning LAVA, spewing from an erupting volcano. Or a STOP sign.

Red in nature was a big warning. Red poppies, red toadstools and red ladybugs flashed like neon lights in the wild, warning animals:

# EAT ME AND DIE.

Thieves were caught red-handed, people with anger management issues saw red as fury filled their heads and hearts.

**Red, red, red** was pressing in around me, screaming at me to **run, run, run** as fast as I could. It was a giant foot stamping down on my chest – squeezing out any little bit of oxygen left in my body. It was just how I'd felt on the Melchior jet, zooming through the sky to an unknown destination, when Alex had told me to breathe into the sick bag. *In. Out. In. Out.*

"Hey, kid," said Violetta Villarne, thumping me on the arm. "You're turning purple. Are you trying to break a record for holding your breath? I can time you, if you like?"

She was bending down, peering at me really close. She was so close her two eyes had become one.

Seeing those evil eyes up close was a totally scary sight and it brought me back to breath faster than a kick start. I took a deep gasp of air. Followed quickly by another. And then another. Soon I was gasping and breathing like I'd never breathed before.

As air rushed around inside me again, saying HELLO to all my organs and blood cells, the red that had been pressing into me began to fade, until the world settled back into a very soft pink. The color of (oxygenated) me.

"No," I said. "I'm okay."

I looked at Violetta's card. I could read the words more calmly now:

Violetta Villarne,

Villains Inc.

Villains for the every day since 1818
CHAOS and DISRUPTION guaranteed

WATCH OUT. VILLAINS ABOUT.

She was looking at me expectantly and holding out her hand. "What?" I said. "Oh, I don't have a card."

"No card?" she said. "What kind of hero are you?" She didn't wait for me to answer. "This is your first Hero Hunt, isn't it?"

"Maybe," I said.

"I know it is," said Violetta. "You've got no idea what you're doing. It's hilarious and depressing at the same time."

"I *do* know what I'm doing," I said. Although I was thinking to myself: *She has a point.*

"Your ignorance is like an iceberg," said Violetta. "Too deep to fathom."

"I know more than you think I know," I said.

*"I know more than you think I know,"* she mimicked. "Listen to yourself. You're so green you could be a cabbage."

"Could not."

"Could too."

I stared at Violetta and she stared back at me. We stared for seconds and seconds. Until she blinked. *Ha,* I thought to myself. *She's not as tough as she pretends to be.*

She pushed me ahead of her. "Move it," she said.

We were silent for a few minutes and then she said, "So you're the kid with the MPs?"

"MPs?" I said.

"Missing Parents," she said.

"How do you know about my mum and dad?" I said.

"Everyone knows about the rift between the brothers in the House of Melchior. How Max and Persephone left the family business and Octavia Melchior has been trying to find them ever since." She paused. "Well, until he died."

She glanced at me as she said this and I thought I saw a different kind of expression in her eyes. Just for a second. But maybe it was only a trick of the light.

"We make it our business to know these kinds of things so we can exploit hostilities and bad feelings between families," she said. "We go where bad blood is already flowing. It makes our job easier. Information is valuable."

"So everyone keeps saying," I said. Albert Abernathy had said those exact words too.

"And besides," she said. "I've heard the story in boring detail too many times to count."

"What do you mean?" I said.

"From Caspian Melchior. Your uncle."

"Caspian?" I said.

"There you go again," said Violetta. "Repeating everything I say. I know my words are worth repeating but try to think of your own. For the sake of your listeners."

"You know Caspian?" I said. "But how?"

"My mum and dad run Villains' School," said Violetta. "He's a substitute teacher there."

"WHAT?" I said.

"Just for a term, while Professor Butterfingers is doing a stint in prison. The prof got sloppy with his safecracking, left a fingerprint on the lock and was nabbed before he'd even stuffed the loot in his bag.

Mum and Dad want him to retire but villains never retire. They just grow older and slower. Then they settle into a Villains' Retirement Home to spend their days cheating at Scrabble."

"What's Caspian teaching?" I said.

"Mindful Villainy," she said. "You know, stuff like Villain Visualizations – manifest the villain you want to be, find your inner villain, etc., etc."

"Caspian's teaching villains to be villains?" I said.

"Why so surprised?" said Violetta. "He's got the face for it. He always looks like he's swallowed a lemon. Besides, you kicked him out of HoMe. He had to go somewhere."

"But VillInc's the opposite of HoMe," I said.

"Exactly," said Violetta. "It's a warped kind of logic. Villains love warped. Besides, Caspian knew my dad from years ago. There was much more movement between the Hero and Villain worlds in the Old Days. They even held a trivia night each year to raise funds for Heroes and Villains in need."

This was a lot to take in. Caspian Melchior teaching at VillInc! Octavia would have been heartbroken.

"But I hear you inherited everything," said Violetta. "Nice work, kid. Showing up just in time to charm the old man. You might have some skills after all, although they're certainly not obvious yet.

**149**

Caspian's still spitting about it. You should hear him. Pounding the floorboards until the early hours of the morning, planning and plotting his revenge. I've seen the flowcharts. They're intense."

# Revenge Plan 10,002

**Target:** Henrie Melchior

**Plan:**
          DESTROY
          DESTROY
          DESTROY
          DESTROY
          DESTROY
          DESTROY

**Mission mantra: Revenge is mine.**

**Villain Visualization:**

I am in the Control Center at HoMe.

I am in control.

I am breathing through my nostrils and filling my diaphragm with revenge.

"Yeah, you'd better watch your back, kid. I'm a villain through and through but Caspian makes even me nervous. And as for his kids…"

"Carter and Finn?" I said. "They're at Villains' School too?"

"Of course," said Violetta Villarne. "They're a few years below me but I can see why you kicked them out. Especially Carter. He looks like spaghetti and I hate spaghetti. And he thinks he knows everything. What a brat."

I thought of Carter trying to sabotage me in the Hero Hunt, even though I'd answered all the questions.

"Yeah, he's a brat," I said.

Violetta and I looked at each other uneasily. This was the first thing we'd agreed on. And it didn't feel quite right.

She laughed. "Don't worry, kid. You're not going to discover I have a heart of gold and we're destined to become best friends. I haven't and we won't. This isn't a kids' story."

"I know that," I said, my face flaming.

"You know what's wrong with you?" she said, turning to look at me.

"No, but I reckon you're about to tell me," I said.

"Heroes think too much," she said. "I can see you thinking now. Wrong is so much simpler than right. Villains drive straight to BAD, BADDER, BADDEST as fast as they can. We love choking people on the

**151**

dust of our speeding vehicles. We don't stop or detour to make sure everyone's okay and that no one's feelings have been hurt. We don't care if we've driven over any big toes. The more the merrier. We're foot soldiers." She laughed. "That's a pun."

"I know a pun when I hear a pun," I said.

"But you didn't laugh," she said.

"It wasn't funny," I said.

"Well, that's another thing," she said. "Heroes have no sense of humor."

"Do too," I said.

"Do not," she said. "But, seriously. My brain hurts even *thinking* about that kind of hero thinking. Are you sure you know what you're up for, kid?"

"If the Hero way is good enough for my dad it's good enough for me," I said.

"But is it?" she said. "You don't know where your dad is let alone what he's doing, what he's become. Maybe he's like Caspian?"

"My dad's nothing like Caspian," I said.

"You believe what you want to believe," she said. "But know this: I'm in charge here."

"Who said so?" I said.

"I did, just then," said Violetta. "I'm older and more experienced. It's smart to know what you don't know, kid."

"Stop calling me kid," I said. "I'm nearly twelve."

"Kid suits you," she said. "And it reminds you that I'm *not* a kid. You have to earn your name. Seems to me you're a long way from doing that."

"What's the plan then?" I said.

"You do what I tell you," she said. "It's simple enough. Even you should be able to do that."

I nodded. I'd do what she said. For the moment.

"And, kid," she said, "there's something else."

"What?" I said.

"Don't get in my way, okay? And I mean *ever*."

I nodded. Twice for YES.

I knew getting in Violetta Villarne's way would be bad for my health.

## Chapter Eleven

# The Key is a Key to a Key

**WE'D ARRIVED AT** the stairs leading down to the basement.

"Why are we going down there?" I said.

"Here's a tip, kid," said Violetta. "And it's your lucky day – I won't even charge you for it."

She pulled a book out of her bag and read from it.

## The Villain's Handbook

**Top Tip 22:** Never ignore the potential of the place in which you find yourself.

"What does that mean?" I said.

"It means *I* know there are lockers in the basement. My hunch is that Agnes's key will open one of those."

"But why? It could be a key to anything."

"Agnes wanted you to come here. And here you are. Just because you can't find one thing doesn't mean you shouldn't look for another." She began walking down the stairs. "Anyway, stop talking. I'm tired of all your words. Villains prefer action to talk."

Ha! *She* was tired of *my* talking. She'd barely drawn breath since she'd turned up with her knitting needle. She was the chattiest villain I'd ever met.

She pushed me ahead of her and we started to descend into the basement, our footsteps *clank, clank clanking* on the aluminum staircase.

As we climbed lower and lower, I thought of Violetta's words about my dad. That I didn't know what he'd become. I knew they weren't true. That they *couldn't* be true. Could they? There was a niggle of doubt worming its way up, up and into my thoughts.

Six flights later, we reached the bottom. Violetta took a zucchini out of her bag. "It's a flashlight," she said. "One of Professor Nineties' inventions. He's a genius at hiding spy stuff in the everyday. You should see his Turbo Tea-Towel Tickler – guaranteed to get anyone to talk. And his Slug Spy Cam is awesome. Nobody suspects a slug of subterfuge."

## Note to you

I'm going to report Professor Nineties to the **SAS – Slug Appreciation Society.** Slugs have rights too, you know.

Violetta switched on the zucchini. "This way," she said, shining it in front of us.

The beam from the zucchini created a ghostly light and shadows shook and shimmied around the edges. We were in a long, thin corridor with a gleaming vinyl floor, like a hospital. Rows of lockers filled both sides of the corridor. I looked behind me nervously as we walked between them, but then I remembered my enemy was in front of me – not behind me.

"Can we turn on the lights?" I said.

"Are you scared of the dark, kid?" said Violetta. She shook her head. "I knew it. What a cabbage."

I blushed. I *was* scared of the dark. And now I did look like a cabbage. A red cabbage.

Violetta was banging on the lockers with her zucchini and counting. "302, 303, 304, 305, 306 … and here it is. 307. Okay. We can turn the main lights on now. We're alone down here."

She flicked a switch and light raced down the corridor.

I breathed in. Light was good. You could see what was what in the light. The dark blanketed everything. Even the bad things.

Violetta took the key out of her pocket. She put it into the locker and turned it.

The door clicked and stuttered open.

Violetta flashed me a smile and opened the locker. We both stared in.

It was empty apart from a piece of paper, sitting on the top shelf.

"I'm feeling generous, kid," she said. Then she frowned. "What a weird feeling. I'm not sure I like it. You can take the paper out. But hurry – before I change my mind."

I reached up for the paper and opened it as Violetta stood close beside me.

A series of numbers was written on it.
We looked at each other.

| | | |
|---|---|---|
| 341 | 28 | 10 |
| 179 | 21 | 8 |
| 282 | 31 | 6 |

The key was a key to a key.

# Chapter Twelve
# In the Dark

**I WAS STILL** holding the paper when there was a **clunk,** and the main lights went out.

The darkness stretched around us like a sea fog – quick, thick and impenetrable. I choked as fright whipped through me.

"What the?" said Violetta, trying to find her bag with one hand while gripping me with the other. "Don't move, kid. Stay right where you are. Where's my zucchini?"

I stood as still as if I'd seen a snake.

Very softly, a hand touched my free arm. Then I felt a light tapping. Someone else was down here. Sending me a message. In Morse code.

I cleared my head and concentrated on the short long short longs ... over and over again.

# MORSE CODE
## ALPHABET

| | | | | | | |
|---|---|---|---|---|---|---|
| A | •— | J | •——— | S | ••• |
| B | —••• | K | —•— | T | — |
| C | —•—• | L | •—•• | U | ••— |
| D | —•• | M | —— | V | •••— |
| E | • | N | —• | W | •—— |
| F | ••—• | O | ——— | X | —••— |
| G | ——• | P | •——• | Y | —•—— |
| H | •••• | Q | ——•— | Z | ——•• |
| I | ••• | R | •—• | | |

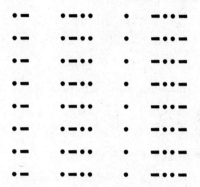

## Note to you

**Stop.** Don't read any further.

Can you decode the code?

Answer:_____

**ALEX.** He was here.

I tried not to gasp or grab him back. He must have a plan. I waited as patiently as I could. The suspense was unbearable and fizzed through me.

### Note to you
Ellie says patience is a virtue but I wish virtues weren't so painful.

Violetta was still trying to find her bag. With a sound of exasperation, she dropped my arm so she could search more easily.

This was our chance.

Alex pulled me back gently and we took a few tentative footsteps.

*Left foot back. Right foot back.*

*Left foot back. Right foot back.*

Violetta had found her bag but was now rummaging around for the zucchini, muttering to herself. "I know I put it here somewhere." My eyes had adjusted a little to the dark but not much. Alex must have the eyes of a cat to be able to see down here.

We moved slowly at first, then faster, and faster. By the time Violetta had found the zucchini with a shout of **GOT IT**, we were running away from her.

"HEY!" she screamed. "COME BACK HERE. THAT'S MINE. NOT YOURS. YOU DEVIOUS LITTLE TWERP."

I smiled as I ran. That was high praise from her. "Finders keepers," I shouted back.

But she was chasing after us at full speed now, her feet slapping the ground at a measured pace – the pace of a runner. I remembered how fast she'd been at Marley's, tearing down the street with the speed of an Olympic Crook.

Alex must have remembered too because he suddenly swerved and pulled me into a recess in the wall. He put his fingers to his lips and we crouched back against the wall, trying to shrink into the space. We were both breathing heavily and I was sure Violetta could hear us. But she was mad, and focused on running faster than us. Speed was filling her ears. We saw her race by us, a blur of anger and movement. She had reached the stairs now and we heard her footsteps, climbing higher and higher, getting fainter and fainter.

We waited. Not speaking until her footsteps seemed far away.

"What now?" I whispered. "We're trapped. We can't take the stairs."

"There's an old service elevator at the far end of

the corridor," said Alex. "Marley's waiting for our signal to send it down."

We ran to the end of the corridor and Alex spoke quietly into his walkie-talkie. "Are you receiving, TIBS?" he said.

"Copy that, MIMI," said TIBS.

"Cargo ready," said MIMI.

"Roger that," said TIBS.

We heard the old elevator grind into life and begin to rattle down six floors:

**1**

**2**

**3**

**4**

**5**

**6**

It reached the bottom with a shuddering thud.

In that split second before the doors opened, a pause that seemed endless, we both heard footsteps coming back down the stairs. Violetta must have heard the elevator too. She'd realized we were still down in the basement and had double bluffed her. But she was too late. And she knew it. She thought *she* was smart but we had outfoxed, outplayed, outmaneuvered her.

It was the best feeling ever. Kind of sizzly and scary at the same time.

She was screaming not very nice things at us (I can't write them down here), her words bouncing off the stairs, but the elevator doors were already opening and there was Marley, grinning at us.

"Welcome aboard," she said. "Your elevator is waiting."

"Let's get out of here," I said. "We've got it."

I was still clutching the paper in my hand.

## Chapter Thirteen

# Deciphering the Undecipherable

**WE STARED AT** the numbers written on the paper
I'd found in the locker.

| 341 | 28 | 10 |
| --- | --- | --- |
| 179 | 21 | 8 |
| 282 | 31 | 6 |

**Note to you**
Remember these numbers. This is a memory test for you. You'll see why on page 185.

We'd been so elated as we'd raced from the Museum of Antiquities and far away from Violetta Villarne, with the biggest clue yet.

But our elation had fallen flat on its face when we'd looked at the piece of paper. These numbers meant nothing to us. We'd been staring at them for hours now. They were dancing in front of my eyes, like a will-o'-the-wisp.

Alex and Marley were slumped in their chairs too. They looked as despondent as me. But then I remembered something Ellie had said: "If you can't tackle a problem one way, try another way."

I sat up a little higher in my chair. "Hey, what did Felix say about his grandfather?" I said, trying to pull the words out of my memory.

"Um … that he died?" said Alex.

"Yes, he did but what else?" I said.

"Um … that he ran up a lot of debts?" said Alex.

"Yeah, that too but something else," I said. "Something important."

"That he liked code cracking," said Marley.

"That's it!" I shouted, jumping up and down and

**167**

giving Marley a great big hug. Marley looked pleased and embarrassed at the same time.

"What's it?" she said.

"The numbers," I said. "I think I know what they mean. It's a book cipher!"

I rummaged through the index of *The Hero's Handbook*. I knew I'd read about them in here.

I skimmed the entry. Yep. I was right.

"Felix said Frederic liked book ciphers," I said. "It's an old but good way of sending messages. And this," I held up the piece of paper with the numbers on it, "is what a cipher looks like."

"Wow. Excellent deduction, Henrie," said Alex.

"Yeah, not bad, I guess," said Marley.

### Note to you

Tough nuts remain tough.

"How does it work?" said Alex.

"The numbers are always in a group of three," I said, reading from *The Hero's Handbook*. "The first number is the page number. So, in this case, it's page 341. The second number is the line number so you count from the top of the page down."

"So, it's line 28," said Alex.

"And the third number?" said Marley.

"That refers to the word in that line," I said. "So it's the tenth word in line 28."

"So that's it?" said Marley, nearly jumping out of her wheelchair. "We've got it?"

"Not quite," I said. "We can't crack the code if we don't know what book is being used for the cipher."

"Oh," said Marley, with a sigh. "Just when we seem to be getting close we're *still* not close enough."

"Everyone using the cipher has to have the same edition of the book," I said. "People often used the Bible, or the dictionary, because most homes had a copy of at least one of those. But it has to be the same edition. Otherwise the page numbers won't match and the message won't make any sense."

"Let's try the dictionary," said Alex.

We huddled over the dictionary, counting out lines and words. This is what we got:

**page 341, line 28, tenth word:** *nothing*
(There was no tenth word on this line.)
**page 179, line 21, eighth word:** *the*
**page 282, line 31, sixth word:** *surface*

"Okay, so maybe not the dictionary," I said. "Or not this version anyway. Have you got a Bible, Marley?" I said.

"I don't think it's arrived yet," said Marley. "All our books are due next week."

"What else could it be?" said Alex.

We were silent as we tried to think of an answer to Alex's question.

In a world with millions and millions – maybe even gazillions – of books, it could be anything.

It's funny how thinking works sometimes. You can think and think and think and think and think and never come up with an answer. But, once in a while, a couple of dots nudge each other and a thought *pings* into a previously dark part of your brain.

Like now.

"*Oliver Twist*," I said, slowly.

"What about it?" said Alex.

"Frederic Fortescue had a copy of *Oliver Twist* by Charles Dickens in his shop."

"So?" said Alex. "I bet heaps of old bookshops have it. It's pretty famous. Dad likes Dickens. We've got a copy of it at home too."

"But I bet it's not a first edition."

"Probably not," said Alex. "Dad picked it up at a chain store."

"Well, I'm pretty sure Octavia had the exact same first edition of the book – with an identical cover and everything – in the library at HoMe," I said.

"Could be a coincidence," said Alex.

"Or not," I said. "Penelope Fuggleton says there are no such things as coincidences."

"She does," said Marley, grinning at me.

"And remember what Octavia wrote in his notes after meeting Agnes?"

I ran to the computer and pulled up the email from Albert Abernathy:

We will communicate via a third party to ensure safety and security.

"So," I said, as my thoughts fell into line, "what if that third party was Frederic Fortescue?"

"He knew all about book ciphers AND he owned a bookshop," said Marley.

"And Octavia obviously knew Frederic because his name was in Frederic's copy of the book. Octavia must have wanted to check it out and make sure it was the same as his book at HoMe."

"So Octavia could send Agnes messages and she could go into Frederic's bookshop to decipher them while pretending to be browsing the books."

"I think you're right," said Alex, looking impressed.

"I know you're right," said Marley.

"What's next?" said Alex.

"We need to get Frederic's copy of *Oliver Twist*," I said, "and see if we can crack the cipher. I'll text Felix and let him know we're coming."

> Coming to see you now.
> Have found cipher. Need
> F's copy of OLIVER TWIST
> to decipher it.

A message from Felix pinged back almost immediately.

> Great. See you soon.
> Bring the cipher.

# How to use this book as a book cipher

## This is what you need:

☐ A copy of *Henrie's Hero Hunt*.

### Note to you

As you are reading these words in *Henrie's Hero Hunt*, you can CHECK this one off immediately. Fantastic work. You only need two more things.

☐ A friend who has a copy of the book. He or she might also be able to borrow it from your local library.

☐ A TOP SECRET message that you do not want your little brother or sister, or your big brother or sister, or anyone else in the world to read.

## When you have three checks...

# CONGRATULATIONS.

You are ready to begin your book-cipher ciphering.

To get you started and to show you how to use the cipher through trial and error (not too much error, hopefully), here is a secret message from me for you to decipher using this book.

| 24 | 21 | 6 |
| 73 | 13 | 1 |
| 117 | 9 | 4 |
| 196 | 14 | 9 |
| 211 | 14 | 11 |

## Good Hero Luck

Or, as the Heroes of Old used to say:

# BENEDIXIMUS

# Chapter Fourteen
# Friends and Enemies

**WE RAN TO** Bleachley Boulevard with joy in our hearts. This was it – our big breakthrough.

My first-ever Hero Hunt. Solved.

Well, nearly. But I had a feeling the rest of the clues were going to fall like dominoes. Ellie always said that once things got momentum, there was no stopping them. They were **off!**

We charged through the door of 52 Bleachley Boulevard like a flash of lightning – all energy and power.

Felix Fortescue was standing behind his desk, waiting for us.

"Felix," I said, rushing up to him, "are we glad to see you."

I took my first deep breath in ages and let out all the fear and anticipation I'd been holding in since we'd met Violetta Villarne. Everything was going to be all right now. Felix would help us. We had the cipher. We were about to get the book.

"You wouldn't believe what's happened since we saw you," said Alex in a rush.

"Yeah," said Marley, "we were kidnapped by an evil villain from VillInc called Violetta Villarne, pronounced 'arn' as in 'barn' or 'yarn.' She was truly despicable and–"

Marley stopped speaking as another door opened.

We all turned as Violetta Villarne emerged from a room behind us.

"Oh, please don't stop on my account," she said, smiling widely. "How wonderful to see you all again and to hear myself described with such spirit. I am touched by your kind words, Marley. Especially the phrases 'evil villain' and 'truly despicable.' What delightful compliments. Is it okay to quote you on my website? I try to get as many personal recommendations as I can."

"It's her," said Marley, pointing a finger. "Felix, watch out."

But Felix was standing very still. As though an evil villain had cast a spell on him. He hadn't moved or said a word yet. We looked at him, then each other. The feeling that something was very wrong began to creep between us.

"Felix?" said Alex. "What's going on?"

"Well, Felix," said Violetta. "Are you going to tell them or shall I?"

"Tell us what?" said Alex.

"Isn't it obvious?" said Violetta.

"No, nothing is obvious," I said, my head pounding with confusion. "What are you talking about?"

"I'm talking about Felix, of course," she said. "He's not who you thought he was."

"What do you mean?" I said, my voice strangled with fear. "Felix. Say something. What does she mean?"

"Oh, I knew it was going to end badly," said Felix, finally finding his words as he fell back into a chair. "I could tell as soon as I laid eyes on you. It was exhausting to see all that hope and trust you carried inside you. I was blinded by it."

"I don't understand?" I said. "You said you'd help us?"

"And maybe I did," said Felix. "For the tiniest twinkle of time. Maybe there was a moment when you brought out the very best in me. But Violetta came into the shop just after you left and she presented me with a much more attractive option. And, unfortunately, that brought out the very worst in me."

"You saw the poster about my parents in the window," I said to Violetta. "That's how you knew I was looking for them. You never had any information about them at all, did you?"

"It's called leverage," said Violetta. "Villains are always on the lookout for it. A girl who advertises for her parents in a shop window is a desperate girl. And a desperate girl can be manipulated. I mean, seriously. Do I look like someone who would have HELPING HENRIE MELCHIOR on her list of Things I Must Do Today?"

## THINGS I MUST DO TODAY
### by Violetta Villarne

1. File my nails as sharp as possible.
2. Paint my room a darker shade of black.
3. Add more evil words to my list of "Words for Villains."
4. Read reports of bad news for inspiration.
5. Buy a cactus. (Spiky like me.)

"But we had a bargain," I said.

Violetta snorted. "Villains don't make bargains, kid. You made the mistake of assuming I think like you. I don't. And won't. Ever."

"So you were never on our side, Felix?" I said.

"Don't limit yourself by taking sides, kid," said Violetta. "Play in the middle. On the left and on the right. The playing field is wide."

"You're a traitor," shouted Alex, charging toward Felix, but Violetta stopped him.

"Stop swishing, Fischer," she said in a low voice. "Emotion drains your brain. You are in a tricky situation. Calm yourself. Think. Assess your options."

"But, but, but," I said, ignoring her advice and giving into emotion. "I trusted you, Felix. We trusted you. And, and … you love peas. Like me. How could you? Why did you?"

"Why not?" said Felix, sighing.

"It was money, wasn't it?" said Alex.

"Predictably, yes," said Felix. "I told you I had debts and needed to pay them. Doddery old Gramps had made a right mess of it all. Every pile of books I upturned hid more unpaid bills. I was never really going to take the noble road. It's too steep and arduous. I didn't have any choice."

"We all have a choice," I said.

"Oh, kid," said Violetta, *tut-tutting.* "You disappoint me. I thought there was some hope for you but I think all that Hero Training has gone to your head. You need to stop reading *The Hero's Handbook.* I bet it's in your bag right now. It is, isn't it?"

### Note to you

It was.

"But Frederic and Agnes and Octavia worked together?" I said. "The way we were too."

"That's what you wanted to believe, Henrie," said Felix, "so you believed it, even when the evidence was screaming otherwise. I was never working *with* you. I was working against you."

*Against you. Against you. Against you. Against you. Against you. Against you. Against you. Against you.*

Suddenly, everything that hadn't made sense before did. Like the click of a lock on a safe that has finally opened.

"You told Violetta about Agnes's key," I said.

"I did," said Felix.

"I followed you to the Museum of Antiquities," said Violetta.

"And you told her about *Oliver Twist* after I texted you," I said.

180

"I did," said Felix.

"And now she's about to take Frederic's copy of it," said Marley.

"She is," said Felix.

"Excuse me," said Violetta, "it wasn't *all* Felix's double-dealing skullduggery and deception. I do have some talents of my own, you know. I was already casing Marley's house but the information really started flowing when you two turned up."

She walked over to the desk.

"Hand it over, Felix," she said.

Felix reached under the desk for the copy of *Oliver Twist*.

She snatched the book from him and clasped it tight.

"Mine, I think," she said.

"That book means nothing without the cipher," I said.

"And the cipher means nothing without the book," said Violetta.

I frowned. She was right.

"This, kids," she said, "is what is called an impasse."

"What now?" I said.

"It's quite simple," said Violetta. "You have the cipher and I want it. That cipher may tell us where the statue is."

"But history will blame Agnes," said Marley. "She didn't steal the statue."

"So what?" said Violetta. "She's dead. She'll never know. She won't be worried what people think about her. She's the *best* person to blame."

"But it's wrong," said Marley.

"Boring," said Violetta. "Right and wrong don't interest me. You should know that by now. But enough of all this talk. Felix, get the cipher."

Felix walked over to me. "I'm sorry, Henrie," he said. "I wanted to be the Felix you thought I was. But I'm not. Give me the cipher."

I looked at Alex and Marley. I couldn't see a way out of this. I handed Felix the cipher.

"Excellent," said Violetta Villarne. "Now tie them up, Felix."

"What?" said Felix.

"I said tie them up," said Violetta.

"With what?" said Felix.

"Well, I don't know," said Violetta. "Use your head. Improvise for goodness' sake."

Felix started rummaging in the drawers, looking for string, or elastic, or rubber bands. Anything.

"I didn't sign up for this," he muttered.

"It's too late for compunction," said Violetta. "I didn't hear you complaining when we were talking about your share of the proceeds."

"That was before you told me to tie kids up," said Felix.

"Oh for crying out loud," said Violetta. "We're not going to hurt them. I love kids. I was a kid once."

I turned slightly to look at Alex. He nodded at me.

I nodded back. I think his nod meant: *I'm going to do something.*

### Note to you
Of course, it could also have meant "I'm getting out of here. This situation is hopeless."

No, he *was* doing something – he was moving back, one small step at a time. He caught my eye again, and tilted his head slightly to the door. I followed his tilt. There was a walking stick leaning against a hat stand. He was getting very close to it. I guess a walking stick was a weapon of some kind. We had to make a move now. Our options were limited if our hands were tied.

Alex grabbed the walking stick and threw it to me.

I snatched it from the air and brandished it like a sword.

Alex picked up the hat stand and pointed it at Violetta and Felix.

Violetta began to laugh. "A walking stick and

a hat stand," she said, between giggles. "Do you really think that's going to help?"

"No, but this might help," said Marley, throwing a vase of flowers she had grabbed from Felix's desk as hard as she could at Violetta.

The throw wasn't good enough to hit Violetta but as she stumbled back to avoid the water and the glass she knocked into Felix and they both fell over.

A moment of confusion was all we needed.

I grabbed Marley's wheelchair and spun it around. Pushing her as fast as I could, we charged out the door that Alex was already holding open for us.

We burst onto the street and ran as fast as we could, people jumping out of the way as we sped by. We didn't dare stop and look back until we had left Felix and Violetta far behind.

"What now?" said Marley. "She's got the book. And the numbers. We've got nothing."

"We have got something," I said. "I memorized the numbers."

"But we still don't have the book," said Marley.

"But," I said, "we know where there's another copy of the same edition of *Oliver Twist*."

"And Violetta doesn't know about this copy," said Alex.

I nodded.

I knew what our next move was.

We had to go back to HoMe.

# Chapter Fifteen
# Bound for HoMe

**ELLIE AND TIMOTHY** Fischer were silent as we filled them in on everything that had happened when we got back to Marley's house. Ellie had turned very pale when I told her about Violetta Villarne. And Caspian.

"Well, at least he's found his people," she said. "The company of villains should suit him well."

But I also had to tell Marley about the confidential memo I'd read in the museum. That was really hard. Marley couldn't believe Agnes was a spy for the Germans. I couldn't either. It didn't sound like Agnes, even though I didn't know her. But I also knew that bad relatives could turn up in anyone's family. And wishing something wasn't true didn't make it not true. We needed proof that Agnes was innocent. Was that proof at HoMe? We were about to find out.

We were getting ready to leave for the airport when Poppy took off her headphones. We all looked at her in shock. We'd never seen her without them. I think she'd been listening to everything we'd said after all.

"You're not going anywhere, Marley," she said, putting the brake on Marley's wheelchair. "Your parents are back tomorrow. I can't tell them you've flown off with a bunch of strangers in a private jet. They're not paying me enough to deliver *that* kind of news."

I won't tell you what Marley said but you can probably guess.

She was furious.

We could still hear her yelling at Poppy when the taxi arrived to take us to the airport.

We promised we'd call her as soon as we had news but I'm not sure she heard us.

As the taxi pulled away from Marley's, I looked out the window. I thought I'd left HoMe behind but maybe it would always lure me back. I hadn't even known it existed seven days ago but now HoMe and the past were wrapping around me like a long shadow, arcing into the present and future. And my mum and my dad? I was still no closer to finding out where they were.

At that moment, I didn't know if I ever would.

The leather seats on the Melchior jet were still deliciously crinkly and, this time, Alex and I didn't have to hide behind packing crates in the hold.

I remembered all the feelings that had rushed toward me on that first journey: not knowing if I could trust Alex, not knowing who or what I'd find when we got to HoMe, not knowing if my mum and dad would be there.

How could two people hide so well for so long? I guess the world was like an enormous sinkhole and if you didn't want to be found there were lots of places to sink.

"What are you thinking about, Henrie?" said Ellie, tucking a strand of hair behind my ear.

"Endings," I said.

"I know how you want things to end, Henrie," said Ellie, giving me a hug. "I want it too."

Ellie had called ahead and arranged for Andrews to collect us from the airport. He looked a little sheepish as he opened the limo door for us. And so he should. I still hadn't forgiven him for lying about Alex being on the plane on my first visit but I guess he was just following orders. Albert Abernathy's orders. I hadn't heard from him again but I knew that I would. When I least expected it. I shook the thought of Albert Abernathy out of my head.

I had enough to think about already.

HoMe looked different when we arrived. There was a big blue banner hanging across the front saying:

# WELCOME TO THE INTERNATIONAL RELATIONS CONFERENCE

"Oh no," groaned Ellie. "I'd completely forgotten about that conference. The place is crawling with strangers."

"Oh, well," I said. "It was crawling with strangers the last time we arrived too. These ones might be nicer."

Ellie laughed. "That's true."

As we walked up the stairs and into HoMe, it seemed to echo with the voices of people who were once here.

I could hear Albert Abernathy showing me the portrait gallery of my ancestors – all those unsmiling Melchiors from the past.

And Finn and Carter in the Hero Hunt, racing up the stairs, trying to be the first to solve the three clues.

I could even hear Caspian in the dining room, telling me that family was everything, and I would understand this when I learned more about the Melchiors' history.

But the loudest voice of all was Octavia Melchior's.

I could see him now, small and pale on the stretcher as he was taken away to the hospital.

The last time I saw him.

I shook the memories and voices away. Everyone was waiting for me. "This way," I said. We pushed open the grand doors of the library and walked in. I led everyone to the bookshelves and the row marked **D**.

*Oliver Twist* was still on the shelf, next to *One fish, two fish, red fish, blue fish* by Dr. Seuss.

I picked up *Oliver Twist* and we all huddled around the table while I pulled out the cipher. Then I hesitated. We had staked everything on my hunch that this book was the one Octavia, Agnes and Frederic had used. But what if my hunch was wrong?

I looked across at Ellie and she smiled at me.

I knew what her smile meant. It meant she believed in me. I just had to believe in me too.

"Ready?" I said.

Alex nodded and started to write down the words as I called them out. "Page 341, line 28, tenth word, 'father, my dear friend Edwin Leeford, by poor young **Agnes** Fleming'; page 179, line 21, eighth word, 'the pursuit. Mr. Giles acted in the **double** capacity of butler and steward'; page 282, line 31, sixth word, 'he been a perfectly free **agent**, is very doubtful: but as he recollected that.'"

It didn't take long.

We looked at the three words before us in astonishment:

## Agnes double agent

"Agnes was a double agent?" I said. "So she wasn't a spy for the Germans?"

"No, looks like it was more complicated than that," said Timothy Fischer.

"Hang on," said Ellie, who had picked up *Oliver Twist*. "There's an envelope paper-clipped to the back of the book."

She was right. *Oliver Twist* was hiding even more than we'd thought.

My hands were shaking as I unclipped the envelope and took out the two pieces of paper inside.

*2 June 1990*

*Dear Agnes,*

*It has been ten long years since you died. And still our last conversation, when you professed your faith in me, plays clearly in my head. I carried this faith heavily for years because I did not know if I would ever solve your case. But, dear Agnes, I have.*

*By chance, some Intelligence documents were found in an old storage locker. And contained within these documents was a page from your case file. A serendipitous discovery with the most profound consequences. My deepest regret will always be that you are no longer here to see your name and reputation cleared, and celebrated.*

*As you requested, I have left this letter for your relatives with the relevant evidence. You intimated that you had already left them a series of clues and that this was to be their end point.*

*I hope one day your descendants will read this letter and know of your great courage. May they embody even a little of the spirit of you.*

*Your Hero Operative,*
*Octavia Melchior*

No one spoke as I picked up the second piece of paper and began to read:

## Name: Agnes Hart

**Operation:** DIG

**Undercover profile:** Miss Hart was accused of stealing a statue of Akhenaten – a statue that in fact never existed.

"Never existed!" I repeated out loud.

"We've been chasing a statue that never was," said Alex.

"Violetta Villarne was chasing it too," I said. "She'll be so mad."

I kept reading.

Miss Hart was subsequently expelled from the British Archaeologist Society. She sought employment at the German Society of Archaeologists and was recruited by the German Secret Service who believed her undercover story that she was bitter about her expulsion and would spy for them against her own country.

**Case file closed:** We commend Agnes Hart for her tireless and exemplary service to the nation and acknowledge her contribution to peacekeeping efforts post-World War I. However, as befits the clandestine nature of her operations, Miss Hart's contribution remains **TOP SECRET** and must not be made public at any stage.

We called Marley straightaway and told her everything. I put her on speakerphone so she could hear everyone.

I started with Octavia's letter. As I read the words out loud, I could hear how much he cared about Agnes and getting justice for her. He wasn't able to do this while she was alive but he had kept digging and digging, until he had solved the mystery. There was a small piece of dried rosemary inside the envelope. I thought of the rosemary in the jar beside Agnes's gravestone. Octavia had put it there. It was his way of saying goodbye and telling her that he would keep searching for the truth. Even after she had died. Because a truth lasts forever. Octavia knew this. And now I did too.

"That's why the statue wasn't on the inventory list of Tut's tomb," said Marley.

"Exactly," said Timothy Fischer.

"Rumors are like a game of telephone," said Marley. "There's not a lot of truth left in them at the end."

"I would imagine that all Agnes's case records were destroyed in World War II and afterward there would be very few people who could verify the truth," said Timothy Fischer. "They kept the chain of communication tight in those days. Only a select few would have known the truth about Agnes in the first place and if they were no longer around, well, it would have made it very tough to get anyone to believe her."

"And she'd have signed the Official Secrets Act," said Ellie, "so she wouldn't have been able to tell anyone what she'd really been doing, anyway."

"Poor Agnes," said Marley.

"No, brave Agnes," I said. "She was a hero, Marley. She had amazing courage, and did really dangerous things. And she must have been incredibly smart. In fact," I paused, "she must have been just like you."

## Chapter Sixteen
# The Girl in the Wardrobe

I **WENT UP** to my room and closed the door. I needed time to think. The last few hours had been a whirl of discoveries. Agnes had been a double agent. Marley had been right. She was innocent. Marley had believed in Agnes from the start.

Sometimes you just have to believe in people, I thought. No one would have known the true story of Agnes Hart if it hadn't been for Marley. But at least she and her family now knew how brave Agnes had been in the war. How much she had sacrificed.

Marley had an ending to her story. She'd found out the truth about Agnes. And her parents were coming home.

I felt a small pang of envy. I bet you know the kind

of feeling I mean. It's like a little pain deep down. You don't want it to be there and wish it would go away, but it stays there all the same, jabbing you.

Ellie said we shouldn't compare ourselves to others because there will always be people who have what we don't have. But there will also be people who don't have what we have. Life was a big jumble most times. Good. Bad. Sad. Mad.

Maybe I was never going to know the truth about Mum and Dad. Maybe there would always be a big empty Mum and Dad space inside me.

My mind was a tumble dryer of thoughts when I heard a cough. From inside the wardrobe – the one Ellie had disappeared into after climbing up the window and rescuing me from the Melchiors when I first came here.

I got up as quietly as I could and walked over to it. I put my head against the door, then yanked it open as quickly as I could.

There was a girl in the wardrobe, hunched in between a fur coat and a tuxedo. Her knees were bunched up and she was resting her head on them.

"I can see you," I said.

She didn't say anything.

"Come on out," I said.

The girl didn't move.

"I said come on out," I repeated.

I reached in, grabbed her arm and pulled her out.

She had reddish hair, green eyes and a smattering of freckles on her nose. Maybe about five and a quarter freckles. She looked around eight or nine.

"Who are you?" she said.

"Who are you?" I said.

"I asked you first," she said.

"I asked you second," I said. "First the worst. Second the best."

She frowned and stared at me.

I tried another approach. "What are you doing here?"

"Waiting," she said.

"Waiting for what?" I said.

"Or for who?" she said.

"Or for who what?" I said.

"It could be waiting for who?" she said.

"I think you'll find the correct expression is waiting for whom," I said. Mr. Tribble would be *tut-tutting* at everyone misusing this.

"Okay," she said. "If you say so."

"Are you here for the conference?" I said.

"Yeah," she said. "My parents said it was okay to explore. But then I heard you coming and hid. I thought I probably shouldn't be in here."

"You're right," I said. "These rooms are off-limits."

"Oh," she said. "Sorry."

But she didn't look very sorry.

I stared back at her. There was something very familiar about her. But I couldn't put my finger on it. I knew I hadn't seen her before but there was something, like a very old memory, stirring deep inside me and desperate to leap over all my other old memories to push and elbow its way to the top of my head so it could scream IN FRONT OF YOUR NOSE.

We were still staring at each other when there was a knock on the bedroom door and a voice said, "Can I come in, Henrie?" The door opened and Alex Fischer walked in. He was carrying a sandwich on a plate, which he suddenly dropped on the floor. I hoped it wasn't a sandwich for me.

His mouth dropped open and he stared at me and then at the girl – this way then that way. Over and over again. Like a swivel head. Or as if he was watching a game of tennis.

"What?" I said.

He kept staring.

"Who are you?" said Alex to the girl.

"It's no good," I said. "I've been through all that. I found her in the wardrobe. She's here with her parents for the conference."

"I'm Hazel," she said, smiling at Alex.

Alex looked at Hazel and then at me again. He looked astonished. And then perplexed. And then astonished again. He did NOT have a poker face.

"What, Alex?" I said. "Use your words."

"I … um," he said. "Can't you see it?"

"See what?" I said.

"You really can't see it?" he said.

"You've asked me that already and nothing has changed so, no, I really can't see whatever it is that you can see. Just tell me what you're talking about."

Alex grabbed Hazel and me and led us over to the mirror.

I stared at Hazel in the mirror and she stared at me. Then, slowly, we turned to stare directly at each other. Neither of us said anything. A fog seemed to be encircling us and I was desperately trying to see through it. I knew there was something I needed to see there. It was so close. If I reached out I could almost touch it.

This may have been one of the only times in my whole life I didn't have any words in me. It was a very unfamiliar feeling. I wasn't sure I liked it. But all my words were lost in the roar of my brain as it powered up like a furnace and scorched everything I thought I knew.

We were still staring, unmoving, when Ellie walked in the door.

She took one look at me and one look at Hazel.

Then her legs buckled beneath her and she fell to the ground.

## Chapter Seventeen
# The Shock of What?

**AT LEAST THAT** broke the staring spell.

Alex and I raced over to Ellie. I put her head in my lap and tapped her lightly on the cheeks. "Ellie. Ellie. Wake up."

"I'll get her some water," said Alex, running out of the room.

"Ellie, please," I said. "You're scaring me."

Alex rushed back into the room with a glass of water and I sprinkled some of it on Ellie's face. She murmured and began to stir. Then we helped her sit up and take a few sips.

"What's wrong?" I said. I felt her forehead. Ellie always did that to me if I wasn't feeling well. "You're really hot," I said.

"I'm okay," said Ellie, sipping more water. "I think it's shock."

"What shock?" I said. "Has something happened?"

"That girl," said Ellie. "Who is she?"

"Hazel someone," I said. "She's here with her parents for the conference."

"But ... but," said Ellie. "But she ... she ..."

"She what?" I said.

"Where is she?" said Alex.

We all turned around to look at her again.

But Hazel had vanished. She must have run out of the room while we were looking after Ellie.

"We need to find her," cried Ellie. "It can't be."

"What can't be?" I said. Ellie was looking wild and excited. I'd never seen her like this.

Timothy Fischer arrived at the door. "What's happening?" he said. "Is everyone okay?"

But Ellie was in a trance. She didn't seem to hear him, and tried to barge right by him.

"Ellie, what is it?" he said, stopping her. He grabbed her by the shoulders and stared into her eyes. "Are you okay?"

"Where are all the delegates?" she cried.

"They've just left," said Timothy. "The conference ended today."

"NO," shouted Ellie. She took my hand and pulled me out the door with her, clattering down the staircase two steps at a time, and racing toward the

**204**

front door. Alex and his dad followed close behind. I could hear Timothy shouting, "Ellie. Wait."

We opened the main door and stood at the entrance. Several cars full of delegates were already disappearing down the long driveway. Too far away and moving too fast already for us to run after them.

I could feel Ellie's disappointment washing through her and drenching me. I wasn't sure what was happening but I was with her all the way. Feeling what she was feeling.

"Oh, Henrie," she said, and my heart caught. Those two words were the saddest I had ever heard.

"What is it, Ellie?" I said. "Please. Tell me."

Her eyes were fixed on the road and the dust from the departing cars, and she didn't answer me.

But, then, she started and cried, "LOOK."

One of the cars had slammed on its brakes and was surrounded by clouds of dust.

Ellie clutched my hand again, twisting it in her own as though she'd forgotten it was attached to me.

A dark-blue BMW did a U-turn and tore up the driveway faster than it should. It swung around the roundabout in front of HoMe, its tires skidding to a stop on the gravel by the industrial garden.

I could see Hazel in the back seat, staring out the window and pointing at me. There were two other people in the car – a man and a woman. They got out of the car and waited for Hazel. They hesitated for a second but then the man put his arm around the woman and propelled her forward. We couldn't see their faces yet.

And then the woman lifted up her face and looked straight ahead.

At Ellie and at me.

Ellie tore down the steps and screeched at the top of her lungs:

# "PERSEY!"

# Chapter Eighteen
# It Begins Where It Ends

**MUM, DAD, ELLIE,** Hazel and I were standing in the courtyard of HoMe. We'd just waved Alex and his dad off in a taxi to the airport. Timothy had to report back to the Super Sleuth Association that his mission had been successful. Parents had been found!

We'd been up all night. Crying and laughing and shouting and hugging.

My mum hadn't let go of me since she had first grabbed me in the biggest hug in the world and my dad had swung me into the air as if I were as light as a cumulus cloud in a spring sky.

"We didn't know, Henrie," my mum had kept saying, tears running down her cheeks.

"We thought you were dead," my dad had said, tears running down his cheeks too.

"I know," I said. "Octavia told me everything. And I had Ellie."

My mum was holding Ellie's hand now. Standing side by side, they looked just like sisters. Sisters didn't need words. Their nonverbal communication was the best.

I looked at *my* sister, Hazel. She was curled into my dad, nestling under his shoulder. She'd had years

of being able to do that and they fitted together so easily.

A sister! I had a sister.

She'd told me last night that Mum and Dad had talked about me all the time. So she kind of felt she knew me already.

We all had so much to say to each other we were strangely quiet now.

Even me.

But that was okay. We just had to wait for all our words. I knew that nearly twelve years' worth would take a while to turn up and I had my notebooks x 11:

A year in the fascinating life of me.

Mum, Dad and Hazel had years of reading to do. They were all in for a treat.

And sometimes you didn't need to say anything at all. I knew that now as I looked at my mum and my dad and my little sister.

Our smiles were as wide as the sun.

I know you'll be wondering what Mum and Dad were doing at HoMe. Well, you're not going to believe this – I could hardly believe it when they told me – it was thanks to Violetta Villarne. I know! I told you you wouldn't believe it.

She'd found some dirt on Albert Abernathy and had gotten him to tell her what he knew about my mum and dad because ... and this is the hardest thing I've ever had to write ... Albert Abernathy had known where they were the whole time.

"Knowledge is power." That's what he'd said to me on the Melchior jet before I'd even arrived at HoMe, and that's what he believed. He'd kept this biggest bit of knowledge up his sleeve. Just in case he needed it.

Of everything that had happened – the kidnapping, stowing away on the jet, Grandfather dying, the fire, Marley, Agnes Hart, Violetta Villarne – this almost felt like the most difficult thing to forget, or forgive. How could Albert Abernathy have kept this secret?

The thing I wanted most in the world.

That deep dark place inside me I didn't visit very often, the place where I stored things I didn't want to think about, was bursting.

Mum and Dad said they had a few things to clean out in their deep dark places as well. We were going to do it together.

But I reckoned that made Albert Abernathy and me even now. I didn't owe him anything.

Mum said they'd gotten a last-minute, mysterious message to be speakers at a conference on International Relations. They weren't told where it was until they were already en route. And by the time they realized it was being held at HoMe, it was too late to turn back.

Dad was still digesting the news that Octavia had died. I could see it in his eyes. He also had to digest the fact that Caspian was a teacher at Villains' School.

I didn't know how Violetta Villarne had worked out we were going back to HoMe because she'd been busy since we'd last seen her. She was front-page news this morning, found in possession of a gold figurine of the Egyptian deity Anubis, stolen from the Museum of Antiquities. I smiled. She'd have loved being front-page news.

I think there were a lot of things we were never

going to know. About how and why it had all happened. Octavia was right. Memory revisits the people we once were. But we aren't these people any longer.

But they didn't matter.

Nothing mattered anymore.

Nothing was as important as this very moment.

A moment I wanted to last forever.

Hazel was still shy around me. I was shy around her too.

I'd never had a sister before. Neither had she.

I loved the way my mum kept looking at me. As if I was the most wondrous thing she'd ever seen and she couldn't quite believe it was me.

My mum.

My dad.

My sister.

I'd never get tired of saying those words.

I had everything I'd ever wanted.

"What shall we do first, Henrie?" said my mum, squeezing my hand. "Today is the first day of the rest of our lives."

"That's easy," I said, grinning at them. "Spray can, please, Dad."

Dad handed me the spray can I'd found tucked at the back of the closet in the hallway that morning.

I'd been planning to do this since the day

I'd arrived at HoMe.

"Help me, Hazel?" I said.

She grinned.

We walked over to the entrance of HoMe and the sign that still hung there and began to spray.

# PS

We found out more details about what had happened to Violetta Villarne. She'd gone back to the Museum of Antiquities after leaving Felix and us to check out the new delivery Lookout Len had been so excited about. (He'd been arrested as an accessory after the fact.)

When Violetta had tried to warn him and yelled LOOK OUT, LEN he'd thought she was calling his name and ran straight toward the police.

I knew that lack of a comma would get him into trouble one day. Ellie said commas were small but significant, just like me.

## The Villain's Handbook

**Top Tip 83:** Temper your villainy and don't be greedy. Greedy villains get caught.

Violetta Villarne had asked me to be her prison pen pal.

I checked with Ellie first. "Well, I suppose that's okay," she said. "She can't get up to much behind bars."

I smiled. Ellie didn't know Violetta Villarne. She'd always be up to something.

Correctional Institute for Villains
Redemption Lane
Holydale

Hello Henrie,

Thanks for writing to me in prison. I suspect they're trying to bore us to death here. And you know how I hate being bored. If boring was a color, it would be gray, and it is Very Gray here. To insult us even more, the beds are hard and the food is bland. If you could put some salt and pepper in the bottom of your next letter that would be flavorsome.

I'm taking a class in knitting (you know how I love knitting needles) and embroidery and hope to discover an Agnes Hart talent for it.

I hope your Hero Training is going well. When do you graduate? With time off for Good Behavior (a foreign concept to me), I might be out in time to attend your ceremony.

They call me ViVi here. I think it suits me. Say hello to your parents for me.
You owe me, kid.

Yours in villainy,

ViVi

## This is your
# HERO PASSPORT

### TOP SECRET
### FOR HERO EYES ONLY

Keep the following pages under lock
and key. Under your bed. Or buried in
the garden in a plastic bag. Do not let it fall
into enemy hands, such as those of your
little brother or sister.

### HERO ALERT

Brothers and sisters can never be trusted.
They will leak your secrets for a bag of sweets.

**NAME** _____

**CODE NAMES** _____

_____

**AGE** _____ **HEIGHT** _____

**EYE COLOR** _____

**DISTINGUISHING FEATURES**

_____

_____

_____

**DISTINGUISHING SKILLS**

_____

_____

_____

**CODE WORD** (to convey imminent danger to
another hero. Should be updated every month)

_____

## PERSON YOU TRUST MOST IN THE WORLD

Keep your friends close

_____

## PERSON YOU TRUST LEAST IN THE WORLD

Keep your enemies closer

_____

## FAVORITE ANIMAL

Find your inner beast

_____

## STRONGEST STRENGTH

Lean on yourself

_____

## WEAKEST WEAKNESS

It's part of you too

_____

## FOOD YOU CAN'T RESIST

_____

## FOOD YOU CAN RESIST

_____

# IT ALL BEGAN HERE

Don't miss Henrie's first adventure!